Assassin's Run

By

Andrew French

Assassin's Run
Copyright © 2012 by Andrew French
All rights reserved

To Chris

Best Wishes

This is a work of fiction. All characters, names, places and incidents are either the product of the author's imagination or fictionalised, and any resemblance to actual people, locations or events is coincidental.

For Matthew, my brilliant eight year old spelling expert and for Alison, who never stopped believing in me.

Assassin's Run

Chapter One

Even though it was summer, there was a cold bite in the air that chilled the large number of assembled mourners gathered around the open grave. The sky was dark and heavy, reflecting the atmosphere in the catholic cemetery in Londonderry. As the pall bearers lowered the polished mahogany coffin into the ground, the elderly priest sprinkled holy water and led the final prayers.

Some distance away, standing amongst the elaborate headstones and memorials, two figures watched silently. One was tall, distinguished looking with a small pencil moustache. The other was a much younger man in his late teens. He wore his coat collar turned up to conceal his face which bore the cuts and swollen purple bruises of what had clearly been a recent and quite savage beating.

As the priest read a short poem by William Blake, the young man looked down at the small silver cross in his hand. Through his sorrow he reflected on just how much he had changed. The idealist of a week ago seeking adventure and excitement was gone forever. He now had to come to terms with what he had become. He was jaded, damaged and would carry the events of the last couple of weeks with him for the rest of his life. He was now faced with what he considered the unbearable prospect of learning how he was going to live with it.

It began four weeks earlier just after eight o'clock on a cold Sunday morning at the beginning of May 1980. The back streets of

Londonderry were quiet except for the occasional barking dog and the fast, heavy footsteps of a man running. Although fit and muscular he was panting hard. He was running, running for his life. Repeatedly he glanced over his shoulder with wide, frightened eyes scanning the empty street. There was no sign of his pursuers. He knew he mustn't be caught. That was something too terrifying to contemplate. He had seen first hand during the last six weeks what would happen to him if he was. Men and women dragged off the street or out of their beds and viciously beaten and tortured for, or merely just suspected of, being an informant. They had a name for such an individual, 'Tout', and now they were after him.

John McMullan wasn't a man that scared very easily. The son of a plumber, he was brought up in Newry, County Down on one of the rougher council estates. As McMullan's approach to education was, at best, hit and miss, at sixteen he decided to join the British Army as a soldier in the Irish Guards. He flourished as both a military man and a leader and progressed through the ranks quickly. Now at thirty-two he was a well respected and a thoroughly professional soldier holding the rank of Sergeant. Although he had served in a number of live theatres during his career and was accustomed to fighting all manner of adversary, it was only these people that truly scared him. They were an enemy the like of which he had never before encountered. All he wanted now was to go home to his wife and five year old son and leave this nightmare behind him for good.

Finally reaching his goal, he pulled open the phone box door and crashed inside. Although the morning air was cold the sweat poured down his face into his thick black moustache. With his heart pounding against his chest and hands shaking with fear and adrenalin he lifted the receiver and began to dial the number. The telephone dial returned anti-clockwise agonisingly slowly after each digit. Poised with a handful of coins over the slot he listened to the ringing in the receiver. "Come on, come on" he urged looking all around him through the filthy glass panes for any sign of movement. His ears strained. An engine! Like a wild animal, his pale brown eyes stinging with sweat, he looked up and down the street fearing the worst. A brown Vauxhall van appeared a few yards away. It was driven by an elderly man wearing a grey cap and white overalls with a half smoked cigarette hanging from the corner of his mouth. As it passed, 'Murphy's Bakers' could be clearly seen painted on the side. The driver didn't even notice the phone box let alone look to see if there was anyone inside. As the panic subsided McMullan momentarily closed his eyes with relief.

"Go ahead." Hearing the female voice in the receiver the soldier opened his eyes with a start and pushed the coins into the slot.

"SBR 122" McMullan recited the identification code as he had done so many times during training. There was a pause and then the emotionless female voice replied

"Stand by."

After what felt like an eternity a familiar male voice came on the line "Go ahead". At last, thought McMullan.

"I'm blown" he blurted out. "I need an immediate extraction."

The disembodied voice was calm and business-like "Understood. Where are you?"

McMullan looked about him for a street name. "Not sure, outside the city walls. Somewhere in The Bogside I think."

"Don't worry," reassured his controller "We are tracing this call right now. Just sit tight we're coming to get you."

"Okay." McMullan controlled his breathing. "The meeting is set for the nineteenth in The Anchor, don't know what time." As he concentrated on relaying the information Sergeant McMullan didn't hear the rusty white Ford Transit crawl to a stop just a few feet away. "And listen" McMullan continued "You were right about...." McMullan's voice was replaced by the scuffling of two men bursting into the phone box. With a dull thud a large black wrench hit the back of McMullan's head. They dragged the unconscious soldier with great proficiency behind them to the waiting Transit.

McMullan's controller knew it was pointless saying anything more. They had got him. He swore under his breath and slammed the phone down.

Later that day three boys, aged about ten, were using the last rays of sunlight to play football on the waste ground close by their council estate. A small factory manufacturing cardboard boxes had previously occupied the land. The owner had mistakenly thought he could stand up to the threats of 'an unfortunate accident' made by the four heavies that had paid him a visit late one night six weeks earlier demanding regular payments. "If the 'Jerries' couldn't beat me I'm damn sure scum like you won't!" the sweating sixty year old war veteran shouted indignantly from behind his desk. One week later his charred remains were retrieved from the burnt out shell of the factory building. The heavies had been right when they warned him as they left "You should be careful, cardboard burns really well."

The boys, finishing their game, began to walk home over the bricks and rubble of the former factory site. Their laughing banter was interrupted when one of them noticed what looked like a scarecrow a few feet away. Running over to investigate, the three boys approached the figure. In the half light of the evening they were unable to make out what it was until they were almost next to it. They peered at the scarecrow, then stood in stunned silence as they realised it was the body of a man. A man in his early thirties, his pale brown eyes wide open. His ripped shirt revealed a blackened torso, the result of a sustained and prolonged beating. The bloodstained trouser legs concealed two broken kneecaps. His black hair was now matted with blood where the 9mm bullet had entered the back of his head at point blank range. Sergeant McMullan wouldn't ever be going home to see his wife and son again.

The following day a green army Lynx helicopter landed at RAF Aldergrove located eighteen miles North West of Belfast. The base housed the headquarters of the 14th Intelligence

Company, a unit of the Army Intelligence Corps. Colloquially known as 'The Det', it was formed five years earlier, its primary role of surveillance and covert intelligence gathering of the Provisional IRA in Northern Ireland. In addition to its Aldergrove HQ., The Det had three other operational bases in the province; Ballykelly, County Londonderry in the north, Fermanagh in the south and the east by Palace Barracks in Belfast.

The Lynx carried Colonel Charles Mabbitt, a man in his early fifties with greying hair and a pencil moustache rather reminiscent of the actor David Niven. On the right upper shoulder of his green combat pullover he wore the upturned parachute wings of the SAS Regiment. Climbing out of the helicopter with one hand securing his service cap, he strode across the tarmac with the air of authority that only comes with senior rank. This was the commanding officer of The Det. Hurriedly, he made his way inside and was met with a sharp salute by Captain Jeremy Noble who led his CO into the office.

Noble was responsible for running The Det's operators in the province. A thin man, Noble was six feet tall with sharp, almost weasel-like, features and parted black hair covering his ears. In Northern Ireland the less an intelligence officer looked like a soldier the better. The Colonel entered the empty office and barely gave Noble the chance to close the door when he threw his cap angrily on to the desk. "What the devil went wrong this time, Jeremy?"

"No idea, Sir. McMullan had been under for six weeks.

Everything had been going well. He felt he had been accepted into the cell and had gained their trust. His information was coming through via the usual dead letter drops and brush pasts once a week, it seemed without suspicion."

"Did he let something slip?"

Noble held up his hands in exasperation. "I don't know, Sir. It's possible, I suppose. I mean, he wasn't an intelligence man; just with us on secondment because of his Irish background. All I do know is I was called to the communications room yesterday morning where there's a frantic call from McMullan from a public call box wanting an immediate extraction."

Mabbitt shook his head and frowned. "It doesn't make sense. He's the third operator we've lost in the last six months. And this one had a cast iron legend - there's no way they could have tumbled him as an agent." He had been playing this game too long not to know when something didn't feel right. Having spent almost his entire career in intelligence, he had worked with most of the intelligence agencies both in the UK and around the world. So respected was he that, when it was felt there was a need for a special intelligence unit to combat the increasing terrorist threat in Northern Ireland, there was only one name on the short-list to head it up.

"He did give us one very useful piece of intelligence though, Sir." Noble said brightly.

"The meeting on the nineteenth you mean? Yes, I read the report on the way over."

"Yes, Sir. As we suspected they're meeting with a new source of funding, a big one."

"Well then we had better do something to stop it, hadn't we, Jeremy?" Mabbitt said sternly sitting down behind a large desk and resting his elbows on the chair arms. "Or Lord knows what they'll be capable of."

"Well, Sir," replied Noble eagerly "I've had a bit of an idea about that." Pulling up a chair he sat down next to the desk and leant forward conspiratorially. "What if the money man never made it out of the meeting at The Anchor?"

Mabbitt's eyes narrowed. "Assassination? I don't think so, Jeremy. The powers that be would never sanction it."

"Only if they knew about it. As far as everyone is concerned it would be just another sectarian killing. Look Sir, I think it's important that these people get the message that their fear tactic of 'nobody is safe' also applies to them. They consider themselves to be untouchable, thinking that they can maim and kill with impunity. It's time that they, and anyone wanting to fund them, discovered that we simply won't allow it, which is why it would have to be done inside The Anchor." He tapped a bony finger on the desk.

"Oh I don't know, Jeremy. I don't like these, what do our American friends call them, 'black ops'? Covert action is one thing but this," Mabbitt paused and blew out his cheeks, "this is something completely different. Anyway, with the ability these bastards have of spotting operators we couldn't get a Special

Forces chap within a hundred feet of The Anchor never mind the target."

"The type of person I've got in mind isn't Special Forces in fact isn't military at all. Furthermore he wouldn't even officially be on attachment to us. We'd train him specifically for this one job. Then if anything were to go wrong we have complete deniability and there is nothing to implicate us. We just cut him loose." Noble's smug expression angered Mabbitt.

"Understand this, captain. I never leave any of my people dangling, official or otherwise. Nobody in this unit is expendable." Noble shuffled uncomfortably. "And where, pray, are we going to find such an individual in less than three weeks?"

Noble smiled slyly. "Well, Sir, I've had an idea about that as well."

Chapter Two

It was Monday, May 12th - just one week after McMullan's body had been discovered. Grantham railway station was a world away from the violence and suspicion of Londonderry. An unremarkable small Lincolnshire market town, Grantham had two notable claims to fame - Sir Isaac Newton, born on Christmas Day 1642 at Woolsthorpe Manor and Margaret Thatcher MP, elected the first woman British Prime Minister the previous year. An achievement that was received with almost complete apathy by much of the town's population.

Amongst the handful of people standing on the platform waiting for the 07.03 train to Harrogate was Michael Prentiss. His black hair blew wildly as the wind funnelled down the platform. This was the day he had been waiting for. Following weeks of interviews, written tests and a medical, he was at last about to embark on the army's three day assessment and selection course. A naturally gifted student, he had received pressure from both his parents and teachers alike to continue with his education and go to university. Prentiss however was adamant. He'd had enough of studying; all he wanted now was some adventure and excitement. He had known for a year that he wanted an army career following an inspiring careers talk from a Parachute Regiment Sergeant Major. This had fired his imagination. Night after night he could be seen running for miles through the streets of Grantham building up his stamina and fitness. His broad back and muscular shoulders were the result of the three hour training sessions, four times a week using cast iron free weights at the local gym.

Prentiss glanced at his watch, five minutes to wait. He knew what to expect. His closest friend and training partner, Mickey, had attended the same selection centre six weeks previously and had successfully gained the certificate that guaranteed him a place in the September intake. Now it was his turn. Prentiss had his heart set on the Royal Military Police. Serving all over the world and considered to be the smartest of men, their motto 'We lead by example' encapsulated everything Prentiss wanted from the army. It was all planned. He and Mickey would be joining the redcaps together. All he had to do now was to pass the selection centre.

Two hours later Prentiss arrived at Harrogate station. Throwing the battered rucksack he had used earlier that year for the outward bound element of the Duke of Edinburgh's silver award onto his shoulder, he jumped out of the carriage and looked about him. As the crowd of disembarking passengers from his train dispersed he saw a group of six young men all about his age. Prentiss had been sixteen for six months but because of his muscular frame and standing just shy of five feet eleven he looked older. He walked over to them asking if they were going to the selection centre. Confirming that they were, their conversation returned to the storming of the Iranian Embassy by the SAS the previous week. Prentiss too had followed the events unfold live on TV. He, like so many others, had sat transfixed as he watched the hitherto little known Special Forces soldiers storm the building. The press had been full of it for days. This 'boys' own' adventure story had captured the imagination in a wave of national euphoria.

It wasn't long before a tall man in his late fifties wearing a dark shapeless raincoat and flat cap strutted up to the group. "Morning lads" he said in a strong Geordie accent. "Are you lot for the selection centre?" Seven heads nodded. Taking a clipboard from under his arm, he consulted his list. "Let's see who we've got then." He proceeded to read out the names, each one confirming his in turn. Replacing the clipboard under his arm the Geordie led the group out to a waiting bottle green Sherpa minibus.

Twenty minutes later it swept through the gates of the large barracks that was the army selection centre. Geordie nodded briefly to the armed soldier standing outside the guardroom and showed his pass. Following a brief introduction in a large auditorium by an overly chummy sergeant instructor, the recruits sat the first battery of tests; literacy, numeracy and mechanical physics. Prentiss found these ridiculously easy and finished quickly. This is going to easier than I thought, Prentiss mused as he looked at the other recruits still struggling with the test papers.

Lunch was followed by an afternoon of gym tests, swimming, running and an assault course. Prentiss' months of training together with Mickey's briefing of what to expect was certainly paying off. Nothing was giving him too much trouble and he was really beginning to enjoy himself. If this was what military life was going to be like, he considered, he was going to love it.

The following morning he was unceremoniously tipped out of bed by a corporal who would clearly rather be posted anywhere else than the selection centre. There then followed another batch of tests in the auditorium.

An hour later the sergeant sent the recruits to the common room to wait for their name to be called for an interview. As the last of the recruits filed out, Prentiss was instructed to remain behind. Once the auditorium was empty he was handed another six page test paper by the sergeant. "I'd just like you to do this additional test before you go in for your interview, shouldn't take you long." Rather bemused, Prentiss sat down and began the test. This one was different. It was more a situational judgement questionnaire than a test. After fifteen minutes he reached the final question and stared at it.

'If you were forced to kill one of the following which would you choose? Father, Mother, Self.' He thought for a moment and circling 'Self' muttered "bloody stupid question" and put down the pencil. Having confirmed that he had finished, he was told to report to the common room and wait with the others for his interview.

After what seemed to be an eternity of waiting the door swung open and a corporal filled the door frame. "Prentiss!" This was it, he thought, and followed the huge corporal down the corridor.

The interview room was warm and quiet. Facing the door, an officer in his early thirties with captain's pips on his shoulders sat behind a large desk. Behind him to his right in the corner of the room was another man. This one was older, greying hair with a little pencil moustache, wearing a blue pinstripe suit.

"I'm Captain Ternant and will be conducting your interview to join the British army." His voice was calm and friendly, his smile large and genuine. Prentiss glanced at the civilian curious as to why the captain had not introduced him.

"Right then," began Captain Ternant, opening a buff document file, its contents almost an inch thick. "Why do you want to join the army?" Having asked the question Ternant looked down, turning the pages of the file.

Prentiss had rehearsed the answer to this question many times. "It's an exciting life, lots of action and adventure, a career not just a job. I'll get to travel the world and make lots of good friends while at the same time having the opportunity to serve my country."

Ternant stopped turning and looked up. His piercing blue eyes looked at Prentiss carefully for a moment. Then the smile returned and he nodded slowly. "Good." He paused. "I see you want to join the Royal Military Police?" Ternant's eyes returned to the file. Prentiss sat even more erect in his chair.

"Yes, Sir."

"What made you choose the RMP?"

"I like the thought of being a policeman in the army. I suppose it sounds a bit cheesy but I have always had this innate sense of right and wrong, upholding the law, that sort of thing. Combine that with the military life; I think I'd be really good at it." Prentiss was feeling confident, prepared.

"And how do you feel about being posted to Northern Ireland?" Captain Ternant sat back in his chair.

Prentiss considered for a moment. "As a serving soldier I'll go wherever I'm posted. If that is Northern Ireland then so be it."

"How do you view the whole situation in the province?" The atmosphere in the room was changing, becoming more serious. The captain's smile had gone and both men were looking at Prentiss intently. He had grown up seeing reports of the troubles in Northern Ireland on the TV news almost every night. As he was about to respond, Ternant asked another question "Do you think, for instance, that the IRA are the freedom fighters they consider themselves to be?"

"No, they're thugs and criminals hiding behind an agenda to bring about a united Ireland." Ternant raised his eyebrows.

"So why are they doing it?" asked Captain Ternant quietly.

"Because they like it." Prentiss allowed a trace of disdain to enter his voice.

The room fell silent. He glanced across at the civilian in the corner who stared back at him, his face expressionless. Prentiss was uneasy. Had he been too candid with his answers? He didn't want to blow his chance. After a few seconds Captain Ternant continued. "And the thought of having to kill someone, how do you feel about that?"

"I don't suppose anyone knows how they will deal with it until they are faced with that situation." Prentiss replied. "But if you are asking me as a soldier would I have a problem with the thought of killing someone in principle, I would have to say the answer is, no."

There was another long silence. "Have you considered joining something other than the Military Police?"

"No, Sir. I've pretty much decided..."

Ternant interrupted reading from a page in the file "I see that you have already taken a number of your 'O' levels early - English, Geography, French, all at Grade A. and you still have a further nine subjects to sit in the next few weeks. That's very impressive." The smile returned. "How's the French? *Parlez-vous francais couramment?*"

Prentiss replied quickly "*Assez bien pour me garder hors de l'ennui.*"

Ternant's smile became a grin "Enough to keep you out of trouble, eh? Good answer". He paused. "Well, Michael, it's like this. We think you would be more suited to intelligence work rather than being wasted as a redcap. We'd like you to go down to the Intelligence Corps depot in Ashford. They can go into it in a bit more detail there. Take some more tests, go through their selection process, that sort of thing."

Prentiss felt decidedly railroaded. "When would I go?"

"Tomorrow, stay for about a week or so; by then you should know whether it's for you or not." Ternant closed the file. "Understand this, Michael" Captain Ternant stood up and walked round the desk. "You are quite an exceptional young man. Very different to most of the people we get in here. You have the potential to do very well. All we ask is that you just go and have a look."

"Alright." He said slowly, intrigued at what was being offered to him.

"Then I think that will be all. Oh and just one more thing, Michael. Due to the sensitive nature of the work it is important that you don't go telling anyone at this stage. As far as your friends and family are concerned you're going to our officer selection centre, okay? Good. It has been a pleasure meeting you and good luck." Ternant shook Prentiss by the hand and returned to his side of the desk. Prentiss left the office, his mind racing.

Once the door had closed Captain Ternant turned to the silent suited figure in the corner. "Well, Colonel?"

Mabbitt's eyes narrowed and as he stroked his pencil moustache said, "He's perfect."

Chapter Three

Donald Boyle was a particularly odious individual both in appearance and manner. A 54 year old third generation Irish American, he was short, stocky and about a hundred and thirty pounds overweight. Boyle was obscenely wealthy, even by American standards. He had made his money buying and selling real estate in the mid-west. By sheer chance he bought ten thousand acres of Kansas scrubland in 1955 to sell to a developer and discovered oil before selling. Needless to say he never sold.

Boyle now lived on a ten thousand acre ranch in Montana, spending his time between the ranch and his fifteen acre beach house estate in Malibu. It was from there he had just returned on Tuesday May 13th, landing at Billings Logan International Airport in his private executive jet. As he crossed the tarmac to his waiting Cadillac limousine Boyle had already started sweating. He brushed his hand through a shock of grey hair that was already damp with perspiration and removed his jacket. He was flanked by two men that rarely left his side. One was a slim figure in a sharp pin stripe suit. A man of about thirty, Thomas Fisher had the look of one of the Ivy League universities about him. Although he had a first class law degree, he was Donald Boyle's personal assistant dealing with all the day to day irrelevances that Boyle's wealth meant he didn't have to consider.

The other man couldn't be more different from the first. Standing a fraction under six feet five, Marcus Hook was a giant of a man. Boyle's personal bodyguard for three years, he had served in the 2nd REP of the French Foreign Legion for the previous fifteen. A New Yorker by birth, Hook's bull neck was as wide as his large bald head and he had the physique of a professional wrestler. As a *Sergent Chef* or Senior Sergeant in the legion he had witnessed and administered unspeakable brutality, both to his enemies and his men alike. If the mere sight of him didn't prove enough of a deterrent he carried a stainless steel Colt Gold Cup .45 automatic pistol behind his right hip.

The chauffeur opened the rear door of the limousine and the three men got inside. Boyle was, by now, sweating profusely. Large wet patches were dark against his pale blue shirt. His two employees had long since learnt to ignore their employer's strong vinegary body odour smell but today even they were struggling. The hour long journey to the ranch was going to be an uncomfortable one.

Seventy minutes later the limousine swept up the drive to the ranch house. Having fallen asleep soon after leaving the airport, Fisher was gently trying to wake Donald Boyle who was snoring loudly with his mouth gaping open. As the car came to a stop the housekeeper, an elderly mouse-like Mexican woman, appeared at the door. As usual Hook alighted first and scanned the area with his trained eyes. Fisher followed. As he did so the housekeeper bustled up to him.

"Please *Meester* Thomas, *Telefono*."

"Go, go." Boyle shouted as he roused himself and attempted to haul his large frame out of the car.

A few minutes later Fisher hung up the receiver as Boyle entered the cavernous lounge slumping down on one of the many white leather sofas dotted about it. Fisher looked concerned. "What's the matter with you, boy?" Boyle looked at the young man's pale face as he was handed a large whiskey. Fisher took a deep breath preparing for the impending explosion; he hated delivering bad news. He knew that Boyle could change from mildly unpleasant to a raging fury in the blink of an eye. The phrase 'don't shoot the messenger' wasn't something that Boyle ever considered.

"That was Driscoll at the refinery. He's suspected for some time that someone has been embezzling funds from the company. After digging around, he's discovered who it is."

Boyle's face got redder and redder as the young man spoke, gazing at him incredulously. "And you knew that some maggot was stealing from me and you didn't think that you should inform me!?" Boyle's voice started almost as a whisper and crescendoed into a shriek.

"I wanted to be sure, Sir, before saying anything." he pleaded. Boyle stared intently at Fisher, his dark eyes burning into him. Finally he spat out his instruction.

"Have him brought here. I think I need to have a word with this transgressor!" Boyle's rage peaked and he threw the half drunk glass of whiskey across the room towards Fisher, narrowly missing him. Crouching behind the desk, Fisher stammered, "Yes, Sir. Right away, Sir."

Leaving the room muttering to himself, Boyle said to Hook quietly through his rage, "Hook, just explain to Mr Fisher that he needs to work on his communication." Without word or expression Hook just nodded.

It was late the following morning when a green panel van made its way up the long drive to the ranch. Coming from the airport it had met the company's Cessna 404 Titan that had flown up from Kansas during the night. As the twin props came to a stop the door swung open and two men got out and carried a large five feet long olive canvas bag between them. With the contents sagging in the middle, the two men tossed the heavy bag into the back of the empty van.

Behind the ranch house, across a courtyard, there stood a large stable block and a barn. It was into the barn that the green van drove, the double wooden doors closing behind it. In the ranch house Donald Boyle was eating popcorn while watching a football game on the television in his study. There was a tentative knock on the door. All the staff knew never to enter without first being invited. "What?" Fisher cautiously entered nursing a bruised eye that was beginning to swell and discolour. Clearly Hook had 'explained' matters to him the previous evening.

"Excuse me, Sir, he's here." Boyle continued to watch the game giving no indication he had heard what had been said. Fisher waited attentively. Gradually Boyle's attention to the game was replaced by an expression of seething rage. Although he continued to stare at the football game it was apparent he was no longer watching it.

"Right" he said slowly. "Tell Hook I'll be there in a minute."

Late afternoon that same day just off the Foyle Road in Londonderry a large Victorian plain red brick building stood set back from the road. In front and to one side was a large car park separated from the road by a wrought iron chain-link fence. The Anchor pub was, to all intents and purposes, just like one of the dozens of ale houses in Derry. However behind the façade of the nightly drinking, smoking and singing was the base of operations for one of the most vicious and radical splinter cells of the Provisional IRA. It was this cell that had been responsible for the most outrageous atrocities of the troubles. It was led by a former docker, now the landlord of The Anchor, Liam Donnelly. A brutish individual, Donnelly looked every bit the former docker with a thick, stocky frame, close cropped beard and tight curly blonde hair. His hatred of the British and all they represented drove him to justifying his ever increasingly barbaric acts of terrorism.

It was five thirty, an hour and a half before the pub would open its doors to its 'regulars', locals that could be trusted. The cell had gathered to hear Donnelly's latest plans. There were six altogether, two women, three men and Donnelly himself. Behind the bar a seventh man watched a black and white monitor located under the cash register. The screen was divided into four and relayed the live TV pictures from the closed circuit TV cameras strategically placed on the walls around the outside of the building.

Next to the monitor was a Browning automatic pistol fitted with a silencer.

"It's time," began Donnelly in his harsh Belfast drawl, "to step up our fight against the British. To do that we need far more advanced weapons and fire power. So, it's time to look to our American cousins for assistance." He looked intently into the eyes of each one of his attentive soldiers.

"You're going to ask the yanks for weapons, Liam?" one of the men asked. "Only we already have two arms caches safely buried over the border."

"No, Davey." Donnelly replied as if he were speaking to a small child. "We need money and lots of it if we are going to successfully complete our next operation. Making armed withdrawals from the local banks is becoming too dangerous; the bloody RUC nearly shot you last time. To be honest it's distracting us from our real purpose. Why take the risk if we don't have to?"

"Shame" Davey cut in "It was a good crack." The others laughed briefly until they saw Donnelly's face then they fell silent. "Sorry, Liam." Davey mumbled apologetically. Donnelly continued.

"To that end I have found us a sponsor, sympathetic to our cause that won't get squeamish when we take the bold steps necessary to bring these bastards down." He smiled smugly as the assembled group looked at each other intrigued at their leader's announcement.

"What is the operation?" One asked as he sliced a beer mat

with a large flick knife.

"Not yet, money first then I'll go into more detail. Our sponsor is coming here next Monday and he's bringing the money with him."

"Bit risky isn't it?" Flick knife interrupted cynically. "Revealing himself to the Brits with a load of cash? What does he want to come here for?"

Donnelly looked at him coldly. "He's of Irish descent. Wants to see his ancestors' homeland for himself, that and there's no paper trail for the Brits to follow when you deal in cash." He paused, and then lunged at Flick knife, grabbing the weapon and holding it to the man's throat. "And if you interrupt me when I'm speaking again I'll make you eat this." He gently pushed the knife until a trickle of blood appeared. "Understood?" Flick knife nodded jerkily.

"Sure thing, Liam, whatever you say." Donnelly released the man and threw the knife on the table.

"Let's start making arrangements for Monday and listen, I want no screw-ups. After finding that bloody tout last week the Brits will stop at nothing to try and get to us. But I'll tell you something, what I've got planned will bring those bastards to their knees."

By the time Donald Boyle walked into the barn from the ranch house the contents of the canvas bag had been emptied. A man lay in a heap on the floor, bound at the wrists and ankles with fencing wire. His wrists were bleeding as the wire dug into the soft skin. Dried blood caked his upper lip - the result of a broken nose he had sustained when he had been approached in the office car park late the previous evening.

The two Kansas heavies were in the process of feeding a hook that trailed on a rope from one of the barn's beams through the wire that bound the man's wrists. The two men hauled the rope until their captive, like a puppet, was lifted upright. Tying off the rope, the wretched man was left dangling, his arms stretched above him and his feet six inches off the ground.

Boyle approached him and stared into his eyes. "What's his name?"

"Bob Emerson." Hook answered from behind the swinging figure facing his employer.

"Well, Bob Emerson." Boyle sneered with a sinister smile. "I'm very angry with you; very angry indeed." Emerson couldn't speak. The Assistant Head of Accounts writhed in pain as the wire dug deeper into his flesh. Boyle gently pushed the man's chest with his fingertips. Emerson cried out as he began to swing back and forth. "How much did he steal?" Boyle calmly asked as he looked up at the man's bleeding wrists.

"One hundred and fifty thousand dollars." Fisher answered from the doorway. He was repulsed by what he was watching and felt physically sick but he knew his presence was mandatory.

"Well, Bob I want it back." Boyle pushed again, this time a little harder. "All of it."

Emerson screamed "Yes, yes it's in a bank in Kansas City! Please, please." His voice trailed away.

"You see, Bob what makes me really angry is that a nobody like you thinks they have the right to steal what's mine!" As Boyle bellowed the last word in Emerson's face he punched down hard on the man's shoulders. Emerson cried out briefly as the wire bit then his head fell forward in unconsciousness, unable to take the pain any longer.

Satisfied, Boyle walked out of the barn nodding to Hook as he did so. "Make sure he gives you the details to get my money back."

"Yes, Sir." replied Hook obediently.

"And Hook, when you've done that, kill him but" he drew closer and spat out the words "make it hurt first." Boyle knew the power of pain, both as a punishment to transgressors and as an incentive to those who witnessed it. With a final glance at the hanging figure, Boyle left the barn closely followed by Fisher.

As the two men crossed the courtyard back to the ranch house Boyle wiped his sweaty face with his handkerchief. "Is everything arranged for our little trip?"

"Yes, Sir. I'm confirming the last details by phone later this afternoon." Fisher replied.

"Good. In that case I think I could do with a little distraction. See to it." As Boyle strode off ahead of him, Fisher's heart sank. Donald Boyle had two main interests in life. One was money and how to make more of it and the other was a proclivity for teenage boys. The distraction Boyle spoke of was for Fisher to get one of the teenage ranch hands for an afternoon's 'entertainment' with his loathsome employer. On more than one occasion a young man's battered body had been removed from his bedroom and hastily disposed of following one of Boyle's more sexually aggressive afternoons.

From the barn the dull thuds of Hook's well placed punches to Emerson's torso with a gleaming set of brass knuckledusters could be faintly heard. These were quickly followed by the poor man's screams as he gave up the required information. For Bob Emerson death couldn't come too soon.

"Sometimes" muttered Fisher under his breath "I don't know why I put up with this shit." Knowing of course, to his enduring shame, the reason he did so was the hundred thousand dollars a year Boyle paid him.

Chapter Four

It was Wednesday May 14th and the train carrying Michael Prentiss pulled into Ashford station. During the five hour journey from Harrogate, Prentiss had gone over in his mind the interview with Captain Ternant he'd had the day before at the selection centre. The knot he had in his stomach was a combination of anxiety and excitement. The previous evening he had phoned his parents explaining that things hadn't quite gone according to plan and that he would be attending the officer selection centre for assessment. Their pride at the unexpected news made it all the more difficult for him. Lying to his parents wasn't something Prentiss ever did but he was surprised just how easy it was and how plausible he had made it all sound.

The train finally jolted to a stop and Prentiss stepped out onto the platform. Making his way via the over-bridge, he found himself at the main station entrance. Parked immediately in front was a green Morris Marina with military plates. The corporal behind the wheel leant across the seat and opened the passenger door. With what appeared to be a genuine smile he called out "Michael Prentiss?"

Prentiss nodded and, as he opened the rear door and threw his rucksack into the back, the corporal moved the cypress green Intelligence Corps beret from the passenger seat.

It was a short car journey taking approximately twenty minutes for them to reach Templar Barracks, the Intelligence Corps depot. The Marina quickly cleared security at the main gate and made its way through the camp to a rather imposing brick manor house. Standing by the dark green front door was Captain Noble who stepped forward as the car pulled up. "Michael," Noble said with tremendous exuberance, greeting Prentiss as though they were old friends. "Captain Jeremy Noble." He shook Prentiss firmly by the hand and ushered him inside. "Welcome to Repton Manor. Good journey?" Prentiss nodded. "Good, good that's what we like to hear. Come straight up and meet the Colonel. Follow me, would you?" Talking hard, Noble led Prentiss up a wide staircase to an office on the first floor. After a brief knock Noble and Prentiss entered. As Noble closed the door behind them the look of surprise on Prentiss' face was evident. Behind an oak panelled desk in front of him was the silent civilian from his selection centre interview.

"Hello, Michael, glad you could make it. I'm Colonel Mabbitt" he said holding out his hand. Prentiss shook it "Colonel."

"Well, sit down young man, sit down. I'm sure you have a thousand questions. Hopefully I will be able to answer some of them." Prentiss sat. "I'll get straight to the point, Michael," Mabbitt continued "I'd like you to join my little merry band."

"The Intelligence Corps" confirmed Prentiss.

Mabbitt sat on the edge of the desk and stroked his ear lobe. "Well, not exactly Michael, no."

Prentiss' brow furrowed. "I don't follow."

"I command the 14th Intelligence Company. It's a rather special little outfit; extremely hush hush known as 'The Det.', short for The Detachment. Our role is to gather intelligence on IRA activities in Northern Ireland. There are about 250 of us altogether, drawn from all three of the armed forces."

"Why me?" queried Prentiss not quite sure how he had gone from applying for the Military Police to being selected to join some secret unit.

"Let's just say that you appear to have an aptitude for the type of work we do."

"An aptitude." Prentiss repeated.

"Yes." He picked up a file from the desk and thumbed through it. Prentiss recognised it as the same file Captain Ternant had consulted the previous day. "You did splendidly well in the psychological tests. You have a natural ability to assimilate new information quickly and you have a flair for foreign languages."

"You mean you want me to be a spy?"

"Oh, we don't use that word around here. It has rather grubby connotations, don't you think? Let's just say that joining us would give you an opportunity to serve your country in a far more positive way than just being an army plod."

"I suppose it wouldn't hurt to think about it. Would I start in September?"

"Ah, no. I'd rather hoped that you would start straight away. You see, Michael, there is a little job I want you to do for me." Prentiss looked at Mabbitt, then at Noble then at Mabbitt again.

"What kind of little job?" he said suspiciously.

"All in good time, dear boy. All in good time." Mabbitt said loftily "First there are one or two preliminaries to attend to then we'll have a proper chat." He looked up at Noble "Jeremy, would you take Michael and get him settled in?"

"Yes, Sir. Michael, would you come with me?"

Prentiss looked at the two men warily trying to make sense of what was happening. The Colonel was clearly not ready to tell him any more but he had certainly whetted his appetite, so he decided the best thing to do for the moment was to just go along with it.

In The Anchor pub in Londonderry, Liam Donnelly was in the upstairs flat. He was relaxing in a large brown leather armchair, holding a large glass of Irish whiskey. On his lap sat a three year old girl with a china doll face, long blonde hair and wearing a pretty pink dress. She was showing daddy her cuddly Bugs Bunny who randomly said a variety of phrases when she pulled the cord in its back. She giggled, innocently unaware that the gentle giant who called her 'Daddy's little princess' was in fact a sadistic killer.

The telephone rang. The little girl mimicked the ring as Donnelly put down the glass and lifted the receiver. He instantly recognised the American accent. "Donald, it's good to hear your voice. How are you?"

"Fine, Liam, just fine. Top of the morning to you." Donald Boyle's voice was bright and cheerful.

"Would you hold on for just a minute, Donald?" Donnelly covered the mouthpiece and spoke to the girl. "Go and show your mother what Bugs Bunny can say, princess, Daddy's talking business." Obediently the child got down from his lap and ran out of the room dragging the rabbit by the ears. As she did so the fixed smile on Donnelly's face disappeared and he returned to his telephone call. "Sorry about that, Donald."

"That's okay, Liam. I'll keep it short - you never know who's listening. So, how goes the fight?"

"It goes well, so it does. The long war by its very name means there are no quick fixes but with your help we can achieve our aim sooner than we thought." Donnelly paused "And you, Donald, will go down in Irish history as a hero."

"I'm just glad to be able to help you brave guys over there to free our country." Boyle's voice was emotional. Donnelly knew of Boyle's Irish heritage and his passion for wanting to, as he saw it, end the tyranny of the British rule of his ancestors' homeland. Since he had first met Donald Boyle three months earlier Donnelly knew exactly how to manipulate him. He was very skilled at exploiting Boyle's patriotic pride and knew just how to get what he wanted out of him.

It was by pure chance that Donnelly had read a rather damning article in Time magazine. It concerned a wealthy oil man of Irish descent who wasn't afraid to voice his hatred for the British Government or his support for the more radical elements of the IRA. It was then that the seeds of a plan to finance an operation that would bring the Brits to their knees were sown in Donnelly's mind. Thus, after an initial contact by telephone, Donnelly flew to

Montana where he spent three days with Donald Boyle, massaging the American's massive ego and playing on his emotions.

"I'm looking forward to our meeting next week, Donald. I'll show you some traditional Irish hospitality." Donnelly picked up his whiskey.

"I can't wait to see that pub of yours, Liam. What's it called? The Anchor? I'll have a pint or two of some real Guinness while we conduct our business."

"That will be great, so it will. I'll have my people collect your party from your hotel and have you here for eight o'clock. Will that be okay?"

"That will be just fine, Liam, just fine. I'll see you Monday."

"Thanks, Donald, you're a true patriot. Bye for now." Donnelly hung up the receiver and grinned smugly.

At Templar Barracks Michael Prentiss had had a busy afternoon. Having first visited the Quartermaster he changed from his civilian clothes into army issue combats. The next three hours were spent on the assault course, firing range and in a detached house located in a remote part of the camp learning the basics of CQB, or Close Quarter Battle, with a handgun. Prentiss was really enjoying himself. This was a new, exciting world and he loved every minute of it. As he was then taken back to Repton Manor for a further meeting with Colonel Mabbitt he decided that he would keep an open mind as to what the 'little job' entailed.

Instead of going upstairs, Prentiss was shown into a large

classroom on the ground floor. Colonel Mabbitt and Captain Noble were both at the far end of the room standing by a blackboard.

"Ah, Michael, my dear chap, come, come in and sit yourself down over here." Mabbitt gestured to a chair near the front. "Had a good afternoon?"

Prentiss sat stiffly in the chair. Despite considering himself very fit he hurt everywhere. "Very good, thanks."

"Splendid. Now I want to show you some slides which I think will help explain what you are doing here. Jeremy, would you get the lights?" Prentiss stretched his aching legs to try and get a little more comfortable as the lights were dimmed. Noble turned on a projector and the three men watched the screen flicker into life.

There followed a series of slides showing in graphic detail the result of bombings, ambushes and murders in both Northern Ireland and on the UK mainland.

""Hold it there." Mabbitt ordered as a picture of a twisted wreck of burning metal filled the board. "That is what's left of an army four-ton lorry that was at the back of a three vehicle convoy. The booby-trap bomb that caused that weighed half a ton." Prentiss had seen images like this on the TV news but never in such detail. Mabbitt nodded to Noble who continued the sideshow for a further ten minutes. The Colonel gave a running commentary as slide after slide showed death and destruction of both military and civilian targets. Finally the projector was switched off and the lights came back up. Prentiss looked earnestly at Mabbitt.

"So, Colonel, what do you want from me?"

Mabbitt picked up a file from the desk next to him. "For some time now we have been watching one man." He took an A4 photograph from the file and handed it to Prentiss. "This man." Prentiss looked carefully at the face of the man in the picture.

"Who is he?"

"His name is Liam Donnelly, operates out of Londonderry, former docker now publican and particularly vicious terrorist. Even the mainstream IRA won't have anything to do with him. We believe he and his splinter cell are responsible for most of what you have just seen."

"So why don't you arrest him?"

"No evidence, nothing that will stand up in court anyway. He's clever this one, clever and dangerous." Mabbitt handed Prentiss another photograph. "This is Donald Boyle. He's a rich Irish-American that has become rather too friendly with our Mr Donnelly for our liking. SIGINT have intercepted a number of phone calls between them."

"And this woolly-headed do-gooder is looking to fund Donnelly's activities?" Prentiss asked.

"Quite so, but I can assure you that this is no well meaning idealist and far from being woolly-headed. He is quite a nasty piece of work in his own right. Has a rather disgusting predilection for young men apparently, if you get my meaning. Nobody dares to speak out against him. Those that do tend to meet with rather unfortunate accidents. Make no mistake this is a very dangerous individual. The combination of Boyle funding Donnelly is a situation we can't tolerate."

"I know I'm beginning to sound like a cracked record, Colonel, but where do I come in?"

Noble sat down next to Prentiss. "We know that Donald Boyle is meeting Donnelly in his Londonderry pub in five days' time. We believe he's bringing his money with him in cash. If this is the first instalment of Boyle financing this terrorist then what you have seen here will just be the beginning. I'm afraid we just can't allow that."

"So?" Prentiss looked at Colonel Mabbitt willing him to get to the point.

"So we are going to send a message to Donnelly and any future potential backers that we will not sit idly by. To that end we intend to kill Donald Boyle when he hands over the money next Monday."

"Makes sense."

"I'm glad you think so, Michael, because we want you to do it." Mabbitt said quietly. Prentiss gazed at him for a moment in silence. Then he threw his head back and laughed.

"You can't be serious!" He looked at both men in utter disbelief shaking his head. Mabbitt and Noble stared at Prentiss with the same earnest expressions fixed on their faces. Prentiss got to his feet. "It's too ludicrous for words. I mean, yes, I can see that killing Boyle will stop this terrorist being financed but come on. Me? Surely you've got your own people or the SAS; they're trained for this sort of thing!" Prentiss paced frantically around the chair.

"Michael, please sit down and I'll explain why we need you to do it." Mabbitt's voice was calm but authoritative. Prentiss hesitated then reluctantly sat. "We have considered a Special Forces operation but the PM would never sanction it. She doesn't like the thought of army hit squads running around Northern Ireland, not politically expedient you see. In addition we are talking about a US national. I don't suppose The White House would take too kindly to Her Majesty's armed forces murdering one of their citizens. That's why it needs to be someone completely unconnected with us."

"That doesn't explain why it needs to be me."

Noble took out a photograph and showed it to Prentiss. "This is The Anchor pub. Looks perfectly innocent, doesn't it? Just like any other city pub."

Prentiss looked "Yes I suppose so."

Noble continued "That is Donnelly's fortress. In addition to all round CCTV, nobody gets in without being body searched and their ID's checked by the doormen. They can spot an operator a mile off. Even the pub regulars have been vetted by him personally and are known to be loyal sympathisers. We can't even get close to the place, let alone take out somebody inside it."

Prentiss furrowed his brow. "Forgive me for appearing a bit thick but why don't you just do it somewhere else?"

"Because you need to see the bigger picture." replied

Mabbitt. "If we kill Boyle in Donnelly's own place it lets him know that we can strike at him where he feels most secure. That's why it needs to be done in The Anchor. Officially our hands are tied but they will know it was us. We will deny it of course but this will really hit them hard and any future would be financiers of terror will think twice about getting involved in Northern Ireland."

"And I'm just supposed to walk straight into this impregnable fortress full of terrorists, having been searched, I might add, march up to Boyle and stare him to death am I?" Prentiss asked sarcastically. Mabbitt and Noble smiled.

"No, Michael. We do have a plan to get you in there, do the job and, most importantly of all, get you out again safely."

"Well that's very good of you. It sounds like I've got nothing to worry about then on, what is essentially, a suicide mission." Prentiss threw the photographs on the desk. Mabbitt leant forward.

"Michael, at least hear us out. We can't force you to do this. Technically of course you're a civilian but I can't emphasise enough just how important this operation is. Once we have briefed you if you still feel you can't do it you are free to leave." Prentiss scowled at the Colonel. "Yesterday you said that you wanted a chance to serve your country. Trust me you'll never have a better opportunity than this." Prentiss knew that the Colonel was playing the emotional blackmail card but deep down he knew that he was right. The horrific images of Donnelly's work were still fresh in his mind. This was a chance for him to make a positive difference even though the mere thought of it made him feel sick to his stomach.

"Alright" he said finally "I'll hear you out."

"Good man!" Mabbitt said triumphantly. "Firstly, you wanted to know why we have chosen you rather than a trained operator. Well, the truth is you fit the legend."

"Legend?" Prentiss looked confused.

"A legend is an operator's cover story, background, supporting documents, etcetera. You have certain skills and characteristics that are essential to complete this operation." Mabbitt explained.

"What skills? I've never killed anyone?"

"The legend requires a young man that can pass as a university student. You will be posing as a French national, Francois Dupont, studying International Studies at the University of Ulster. You speak fluent French."

"Magee College at the University in Londonderry has a number of foreign students so you won't look out of place." added Noble.

Mabbitt continued. "The Anchor isn't far from the university and Donnelly allows students in there to maintain the appearance of legitimacy. He also uses it as a recruiting ground for the cause."

"Impressionable minds and all that." Noble smiled.

"Okay, so that gets me inside but I'm still unarmed. How do I kill Boyle?" Prentiss asked. "Poisoned umbrella?"

"Oh, very droll. No, you will have a concealed gun…"

"Wait a minute didn't you say that I would be searched at the door?" interrupted Prentiss.

Mabbitt grinned "Glad to see that you are paying attention, Michael. Yes, you will be searched at the door but we have a rather clever way of smuggling a gun in with you."

"He needs to be shot. Anything more subtle won't have the same impact." Noble added. Prentiss didn't press the point but allowed the Colonel to continue with his briefing.

"At precisely 9.30pm on Monday evening you will walk towards Boyle. As you do so there will be a commotion at the pub door. This will be the RUC arriving in their usual robust fashion having been alerted by an anonymous telephone call about a young man fitting your description causing a disturbance in the pub."

"And that will be your window of opportunity." Noble interjected.

"And your escape route. The RUC officers will be looking for you so you will only have a few seconds. Walk slowly to within about ten feet of Boyle then, and this is the tricky bit, you will need to shoot his bodyguard and then Boyle, throw the gun and surrender before the RUC shoot you." Mabbitt paused.

"Whoa, wait a minute. What bodyguard?" Prentiss exclaimed. Noble reached into the file and produced a photograph.

"Bloody hell." muttered Prentiss as he studied the picture of Marcus Hook. "He's...big."

"Michael, dear boy, you haven't got to fight him, just shoot him." Mabbitt said reassuringly. "But you will have to work quickly. You'll have two seconds at most to fire, drop the gun, then in true French style, surrender. The RUC will be on you like a ton of bricks. I'm afraid they'll be a little rough and you will get a few bumps and bruises but trust me, it will get you out of there alive."

"So just to sum up then." Prentiss said cheerfully. "Completely unofficially, you want me to shoot two men in front of one of the most vicious terrorists in the country. And, providing he doesn't shoot me and oh, the local police don't shoot me, I'm going to get a good beating then arrested and dragged away."

"That's the thrust of it, Michael, yes." Mabbitt said.

"I haven't heard how I'm going to avoid spending the next twenty-five years in prison yet."

"We'll extract you before you get to the police station." Noble said.

"You've got it all worked out haven't you?" Prentiss sat quietly in the chair, his mind racing. He didn't know if it was the adrenalin surging through his body or the nervous energy that made him nauseas. All he did know was that he was feeling wildly patriotic. He found himself in a position to make a positive contribution in the fight against the scourge of terrorism in Northern Ireland. How many times, he thought to himself, had he sat and watched a news report about yet another atrocity in the name of the cause wishing he could do something about it. Well, now he could.

Finally Colonel Mabbitt spoke earnestly. "Well, Michael, it's up to you. If there was any other way believe me we'd take it, but there isn't. I know it's dangerous and we're asking a lot but this operation has to succeed. Will you do it?"

Prentiss looked again at the photographs of Donnelly, Hook and Boyle. Captain Noble glanced across at Mabbitt and nodded. They both knew he was in.

Chapter Five

Captain Jeremy Noble had been flown back to RAF Aldergrove by army Gazelle helicopter from Templar Barracks following a two hour private meeting with Colonel Mabbitt. It was now seven thirty on a wet and miserable Thursday morning and Noble was sat at his desk yawning. In his role co-ordinating The Det's operations in Northern Ireland, he was one of only a handful of personnel with a Level One password for the army's 3702 computer system. This Level One clearance gave him full access to all intelligence files on the system. These files ranged from the RUC Special Branch Intelligence reports, called SB50's, to MI5 and MI6 material, in addition to The Det's operational files. As the Security Services were running very few agents in the province, much of the intelligence came from RUC informants and The Det's own surveillance activities.

The working relationship between the intelligence agencies was, at best, a fragile one. The RUC Special Branch didn't want their SB50 Intelligence reports put onto the army computer, so the army didn't tell them that they did so. MI5 were technically responsible for counter intelligence in the UK. This was focused primarily on the mainland although they did maintain a strong presence in the province. It was The Det that had been formed with the sole purpose of gathering intelligence on terrorist activity in Northern Ireland and they were very good at it.

The previous evening Michael Prentiss had been escorted to the accommodation block via the mess hall by an Intelligence

Corps Corporal whilst Mabbitt and Noble remained in the classroom in Repton Manor. The Colonel was pensive and subdued as he thumbed through Prentiss' file. Noble on the other hand was busily fixing the photographs of the main protagonists to the blackboard beneath the words 'Operation Ares' - the codename designated for the mission. This was the mission profile where all the details of the operation were located in preparation for Prentiss' first intensive briefing the following morning.

Noble glanced over at Mabbitt and noticed his serious expression.

"Having second thoughts about Prentiss, Sir?" he asked breaking the silence. Mabbitt turned the page in the file.

"Six months ago Prentiss was on the Duke of Edinburgh's Award expedition in the Brecon Beacons to gain his silver medal. You know, outward bound that type of thing. He was in a group of five young men somewhere near Pen y fan. A couple of hours into the trek the weather closed in. We all know how delightful the weather can be on the Brecon's in November, don't we?" Both men had completed the SAS selection course in that same area.

"Lovely scenery" Noble replied dryly. "When you can see it."

"Quite." Mabbitt continued returning to the file "One of his party fell and broke his leg, compound fracture, very nasty. It wasn't long before the lad started going into shock. One of the others had first aid experience and did what he could but it was all looking a bit bleak." Noble put down the chalk.

"So what happened?"

"Having had the presence of mind to get a fix on their position while there was still enough visibility to do so and in absolutely atrocious conditions, freezing rain and dense fog, our Michael set out alone and navigated his way by compass to the checkpoint to get help. Saved the boy's life."

"Impressive."

Mabbitt closed the file. "Anyone that can demonstrate that sort of selfless courage and determination will have what it takes to do this. No, Jeremy, no second thoughts." He stood and examined the blackboard. "Have the SIGINT telephone intercepts been put onto the computer?"

"Yes, Sir, this morning."

"Good, you had better go and do a bit of tidying. Be back here by eighteen hundred tomorrow." Mabbitt looked at Noble intently.

"Yes, Sir, I'll take care of it."

The following morning, just before eight, Captain Noble made his way down the long corridor that led to the computer room. The room had half a dozen computer terminals set out on individual workstations. The quiet tapping of the keyboards were all that could be heard as Noble entered the room having first entered the four digit entry code. Momentarily four pairs of eyes looked up impassively and then returned to their inputting duties. He walked into a small office in which another computer terminal was located and sat in front of the monitor screen.

All information pertaining to intelligence gathering activities in Northern Ireland is automatically put onto the army computer system. As this was to be a completely unofficial operation, the telephone calls intercepted by SIGINT, or Signals Intelligence, needed to be erased. This was the 'tidying' Mabbitt had referred to. Noble accessed the computer system using his Level One password and searched for the relevant file. He casually looked about him periodically to ensure that he wasn't being overlooked. After a few seconds he located the intercept file and, with a final cautionary look around, he pressed the delete key. The file disappeared instantly. Noble spent a further ten minutes examining the system then logged off and left the computer room.

In Templar Barracks, following a somewhat, but understandably, restless night, Michael Prentiss was meeting the team Colonel Mabbitt had assembled to prepare him for the operation. Prentiss found himself once again in the large classroom in Repton Manor. The manor was now designated 'off limits' to everyone except those that had been personally cleared by Mabbitt. The room had been reconfigured so that there was now a semi circle of chairs behind desks in front of the blackboard. Behind the semi circle there was a large table in the middle of the room on which maps, floor plans and photographs were laid out. Prentiss crossed the room, his boots echoing on the polished wooden parquet floor.

Assassin's Run

"Good morning, Michael" greeted Mabbitt standing in front of the blackboard. "Come and meet everyone." He gestured to an empty chair. Obediently Prentiss sat down. He looked at the occupants of three other chairs. "Right let's make a start." Mabbitt clapped his hands and rubbed them together. "Unfortunately Captain Noble has had to pop out but he'll be back tomorrow. These three people are specialists in their particular fields. They are going to spend the next few days preparing you in every aspect of Operation Ares." He turned and pointed to the words titled at the top of the blackboard.

"So, introductions then. Firstly we have Staff Sergeant Richard Jordan. Before coming to us Richard spent twelve years in the 22nd Special Air Service Regiment and will be responsible for your weapons training." Prentiss looked at the man that was seated furthest away from him. Jordan nodded with the merest hint of a smile.

"Next to him we have Lieutenant Katie Preston, language specialist. She will be coaching you until you are comfortable with speaking French fluently." Prentiss stared at the beautiful young woman. She was twenty-six, her long blonde hair was tied back in a pony tail and she had the clearest blue eyes he had ever seen. Wow, he thought.

"Bonjour Michael, agreable pour vous rencontrer." She spoke quietly with a soft Parisian accent. Prentiss stared at the young woman until he was aware of everyone's eyes on him. He cleared his throat.

"*Gentil de vous rencontrer aussi.*" Lieutenant Preston smiled as Prentiss felt his cheeks begin to glow. Mabbitt pointed towards the occupant of the third chair, a greying middle aged man wearing half moon spectacles.

"Last but not least we have Dr Simon Alexander. The good doctor is our psychiatrist."

"Hello, Michael," greeted Dr Alexander warmly in a strong Glaswegian burr. "I'm here if you need anyone to talk to at any time about anything."

Prentiss recoiled "Thanks, Doc, but I don't think I'm ready for a shrink just yet."

Alexander held out his hand and looked at Prentiss square in the face over his spectacles. "What you are being asked to do will involve some serious psychological issues. It is my job to help you to deal with them. Don't underestimate for one minute that this is going to be easy for you. If it were, you would be a psychopath, making you unstable and therefore useless to us. Make no mistake, Michael, you are going to have to live with the ramifications of your actions." The room fell silent at the doctor's words. It pulled into sharp focus in Prentiss' mind, possibly for the first time, what he was going to do.

"Michael" Colonel Mabbitt said. Prentiss was deep in thought. "Michael" after a few seconds Prentiss became aware that he was being spoken to and responded by looking up at him. "Okay?" They all looked at Prentiss carefully, their combined years of experience telling in their eyes. Prentiss smiled and nodded.

"Let's get on with it."

The phone rang behind the bar in The Anchor and was answered by Liam Donnelly. He immediately recognized the muffled voice on the other end.

"We need to meet. Usual place, one o'clock." Without replying Donnelly replaced the receiver thoughtfully. He glanced at his watch, twelve fifteen. Reaching under the counter he picked up the Browning 9 millimetre automatic pistol and pushed it into his waistband in the small of his back beneath his jacket.

"Davey!" he called. Almost instantly a face appeared at the door to the cellar. "I've got to go out for a couple of hours. Look after things until I get back."

"Sure thing, Liam." Donnelly grabbed the keys to the brown Vauxhall Viva parked outside. Before getting in he knelt down and looked carefully underneath the car. Methodically he scanned beneath the vehicle from front to back. He then unlocked the driver's door, leant inside and sprung the bonnet. Holding it open with one hand he inspected the engine compartment. Satisfied that there were no explosive devices he dropped the bonnet shut. Donnelly performed this precautionary routine whenever the vehicle had been left unattended. It was a practice that had saved his life the previous year. Flicking the key in the ignition Donnelly drove the Viva from the car park and made his way out of the city.

It was five minutes to one when the Viva splashed to a stop

in a puddle at the side of a deserted muddy country lane. Donnelly switched off the engine and got out of the car. He looked up. The slate grey sky threatened rain and there was a chill from the gusting northerly wind. The only sounds were from a handful of inquisitive cows grazing in the adjacent field punctuated by the occasional call of a wood pigeon.

Donnelly climbed over the wooden fence and casually strolled across the field towards a small area of woodland. The fallen twigs cracked beneath his shoes as he made his way deeper into the wood. A few minutes later he arrived at a large fallen tree in the centre of a clearing. Sitting on the trunk, Donnelly took out a pack of cigarettes and lit one.

"So what's so urgent it couldn't wait until next week?" He asked watching the cigarette smoke rise into the air. From fifteen feet behind him, concealed amongst the trees a voice replied

"A little bird tells me that you have made a new friend."

Donnelly didn't look round he simply took another draw on his cigarette. "What of it?"

"Rumour has it that your new friend is going to have a nasty accident in your little kingdom on Monday night." Donnelly stiffened but said nothing. "However" the voice continued "that may be to our advantage."

"What do you mean?"

"You sometimes have to sacrifice a pawn or two to win the game."

"Explain." Donnelly threw the cigarette in front of him as the disembodied voice laid out his plan.

"You're a devious little bastard, so you are." Donnelly pronounced ten minutes later.

"Let's just say I see things a little clearer having the fortune of not being hindered by patriotic blinkers."

"So what do you believe in?" Donnelly's question was met by silence. He waited for a moment then turned and scanned the trees. The owner of the voice had gone.

Prentiss had spent the day receiving an intensive briefing by Colonel Mabbitt on Operation Ares. His mind was sharp. He found the strategy development and minute planning exhilarating. He was beginning to feel very comfortable in this clandestine world of secrecy and subterfuge. Every subtle nuance and variation had been covered. The aspect that caused greatest amusement was how the gun was to be smuggled inside the pub. Having been asked the question by Prentiss, Mabbitt reached inside a briefcase and triumphantly held up the solution. "Your gun will be carried in these." Prentiss stared incredulously at a pair of black cotton boxer shorts.

"You know, Colonel" Prentiss finally said. "You people never fail to surprise me. Just when I thought I'd seen everything, you give me a gun in a pair of pants."

"Ah you may mock, my boy, but this garment has been specially designed for this operation."

"I'll need more than an operation if the gun goes off in

those." Mabbitt laughed and handed the shorts to Prentiss.

"Inside is a small compartment that will hold the gun in place." he explained. "The compartment is hidden behind this padded section that has the outline of a gentleman's genitals formed onto it."

"So when I get searched they will feel this and not the gun."

"Quite so. Rather ingenious, don't you think?"

"It's not a big gun, is it?" Prentiss asked hopefully.

"Okay I think that's enough for now." Mabbitt smiled as Jordan entered the room. "Ah, Richard just in time. Michael, it's time for you to become acquainted with the counterpart to your underwear."

The former SAS sergeant led Prentiss down a flight of stairs into a basement firing range. The room was about a hundred feet long and lined on three sides by sandbags piled from floor to ceiling. At the far end from where Prentiss and Jordan were standing were a number of silhouette targets. The two stood behind a long table on which lay a variety of handguns, boxes of ammunition, ear defenders and all manner of gun cleaning paraphernalia. Jordan picked up a small handgun. "Generally we use Walther PPK's in this unit but I'm giving you the Beretta 7.65. It's been around for years and is very reliable. It won't let you down." He gave the small, shiny black pistol to Prentiss. It fitted snugly in his hand.

"It's heavier than I imagined."

"You'll soon get used to it." His voice was business-like and without warmth. He handed Prentiss the magazine. "Put this in and pull the slide back." Having been instructed the previous day Prentiss knew what to do. "Right let's try a few rounds so you can get the feel of it." Jordan nodded towards the silhouette targets. "In your own time, fire when ready." There were seven loud sharp cracks as the weapon jumped into life. "It looks like we've got some work to do." Jordan sneered as he peered at the undamaged target. Irritated, Prentiss pulled off the ear defenders he had put on before firing and, throwing them angrily on the table, turned on Jordan.

"Well I'm not going to be shooting him from the bloody car park, am I?"

"Let's just try and see if we can get a basic level of competence shall we?"

Prentiss put down the gun. "Have you got a problem with me?"

Jordan stared coldly at him "Now, listen to me, boy. I've killed people all over the world, Somalia, Dhofar, Northern Ireland and they were just the official jobs. I've seen too many friends, highly trained soldiers, cut down by the likes of Liam Donnelly. I don't think you've got the first idea what you're getting yourself into. It takes years of training to carry out an operation like this. You were at school last week for Christ sake! I don't know what the old man's thinking of getting you involved in this. It'll take a bloody miracle to pull this off."

Prentiss considered for a moment. "Thanks for the vote of

confidence. I suppose you think that it should be you doing it next week. Unfortunately for both of us whoever came up with this insane plan decided it had to be me." He looked carefully at Jordan. "Yes, I'm sure that there are others that could do this much better than me and no, I've no idea how I'm going to cope with it but I do know that I'm prepared to try. The Colonel's relying on me to do it. I can't walk away from this and I won't." He picked up the gun again. "So you'd better teach me everything you can without the sarcasm, and we'll both pray for a bloody miracle."

Two hours and five hundred rounds later Prentiss was improving considerably. Jordan had left him to practice alone, tapping the boxes of ammunition as he went stating, "I want this lot to be gone by the time I get back."

As the gun's slide locked back showing the magazine was now empty again, Prentiss was aware of someone behind him. He looked over his shoulder. Lieutenant Preston was leaning in the doorway with her arms folded. She stepped into the room. "Not bad."

"Getting there." replied Prentiss turning his attention once more to his gun. He took the empty magazine out and started reloading.

"I hear you were planning on joining the Military Police."

"Yep, before your boss decided that I was the chosen one," he said smiling.

"I started out in the RMP, went straight in after Sandhurst. It's funny I never thought I'd end up in intelligence, let alone this lot."

"So why did you?" Prentiss stopped reloading.

"It was while I was on a posting to Germany. I was assigned to Colonel Mabbitt's close protection detail when he was on a visit. He must have seen something he liked in me."

"I'll bet he did." Prentiss interrupted. Preston pulled a face and continued.

"Anyway, shortly after I was asked if I wanted a transfer to The Det and I said yes. I was told to put my uniform in mothballs because I wouldn't be needing it any more. That was two years ago."

"Ever regretted it, Lieutenant?" Prentiss asked, curious as to her motives for joining.

"Never, and it's Katie. We don't use ranks much in the unit. It's quite informal really - not like the regular army at all."

"I must admit it all seems pretty relaxed but I thought that was just for my benefit." Preston laughed a bright, infectious, sexy laugh and Prentiss fell even more in love with her.

"No, everyone's friendly. Well, all except Captain Noble. He's a funny one, really private, doesn't like mixing with the others. Sticks pretty close to the Colonel."

"What's his background?"

"Not sure. I know he was on secondment to MI5 for quite a while before he joined The Det."

"Seems okay though." Prentiss said having loaded the magazine and pushed it into the butt of the gun. Preston forced a smile.

"Yes I suppose so."

"You don't think so?" Prentiss could clearly see that there was something else.

"Well, it's just… I don't know; there's something about him. Nothing I can put my finger on. He's just a bit creepy." She paused for a moment and looked at Prentiss carefully. "Are you okay, Michael? With all this I mean?" Prentiss let his guard down a little.

"I know what you are all thinking. I can see it in your faces. I'm untrained and inexperienced and everybody doubts that I can do it. To be honest with you, I don't know if I can. I do know that I'm scared, but I suppose I'm more scared of not trying. So, I'm going to put on those ridiculous pants and I'm going to try and by Tuesday we'll know if I can do it, won't we?"

"Michael, listen…." Preston said but stopped abruptly as Jordan appeared.

"How's our boy doing?" He said standing behind them. Prentiss pulled back the slide, aimed and fired seven shots into the centre of the target. Preston turned to Prentiss admiringly

"Oh I think he's doing alright."

Chapter Six

Donald Boyle's Cadillac limousine made its way through the soaring Montana landscape on its return journey from the city of Billings. Alone in the rear sat Thomas Fisher, his hand resting casually on a large leather attaché case on the seat next to him. It was mid morning and he gazed out of the window at the Beartooth Mountains in the distance. Spring was a short season in Montana. The harsh, dry winter had abated and the hot summer beckoned. Soon the tourists would be flocking to the Yellowstone National Park and the Little Big Horn Battlefield National Monument.

Fisher had been driven into Billings quite early that morning, arriving at the Broadwater National Bank at nine thirty. He had been met in the lobby by the Manager, a rather obsequious character by the name of Floyd Randall the Third.

"Mr Fisher," he bubbled "how lovely to see you again. How are you?"

"Fine" he replied sharply "Is everything ready?" It was probably because Fisher was kept subjugated by Boyle that he relished the power and authority he had over this toadying little man.

"Yes, yes, Mr Fisher. If you would like to come through to my comfortable office we can attend to the paperwork." Talking hard, Randall led Fisher from the lobby through to his office. "I must say I was surprised when I got your call. It is very unusual to withdraw such a large amount in cash. I can't imagine what Mr Boyle would want with such a sum."

Fisher didn't reply to Randall's twittering; he simply sat in the chair and watched as the Manager took the withdrawal form from his desk drawer.

"I have prepared the documentation for you, Mr Fisher." He pushed the paper over the polished desk and placed it in front of Fisher. "If you would just care to sign for me." As Fisher signed the bottom of the form with a flourish Randall tapped the intercom on his desk. "Have Mr Boyle's money brought through for Mr Fisher."

Randall sat awkwardly behind his desk for a minute or so smiling nervously at Fisher. Finally there was a sharp rap on the door and Randall jumped with startled relief. The door opened and a uniformed security guard entered carrying a large metal strong box. Randall stood "Just put it on the desk." Obediently the guard placed the box on the desk and left. Fisher picked up the attaché case and placed it next to the box. Placing the neat bundles of thousand dollar bills into the case, the bank manager counted the money as he put it in.

"Five hundred thousand dollars." Randall announced as the last bundle was transferred. He looked at Fisher waiting for some kind of reaction to the fortune in cash in front of him. There was none. Fisher merely shut the case and extended his hand.

"Thank you, Mr Randall. Good morning." Turning on his heel Fisher flung open the door and swept out of the lobby and into the waiting limousine leaving the hapless manager behind him. As he continued to gaze out of the car window he could still hear

Boyle's voice that morning

"Go and get my money and keep your mouth shut!"

Thirty minutes later the limousine made its way up to the ranch house. It pulled up next to a black sedan. As Fisher walked up the steps to the house he looked back at the unfamiliar car. As he went inside a very tall, muscular figure in a dark suit was emerging from Boyle's study. Marcus Hook stood in the hallway and watched the man leave. The two men briefly made eye contact but the suit returned Hook's stare with a contemptuous sneer. Boyle stood in the study doorway "Fisher, get your ass in here!" he yelled as he turned and disappeared from view.

"Oh crap" Fisher mumbled as he walked into the study. He stood just inside the room clutching the attaché case. "I have the cash, Sir." Boyle was pacing back and forth behind his desk like a caged animal, running his fingers repeatedly through his hair. He stared at the floor in front of him, his eyes wide with anger and frustration. Suddenly he picked up a large brown envelope from the desk. Ripping it in two, then four he threw the pieces back onto the desk. Snatching up a knife that lay on the desk he began stabbing at the pieces in a wild frenzy. Throwing the knife into the room he then turned and punched the wall letting out a thundering yell. Fisher was quite used to seeing his employer's temper but this went further than he had ever seen before. It was impossible to know what to do in such a situation. If he left the room without permission or remained and said the wrong thing there would be painful consequences. He didn't have to wait long however before

Boyle turned to him, his face soaked in sweat. "What!" he said beginning to regain his composure.

"I have the cash." Fisher held up the case. Boyle squinted as he focused on it.

"Any problems at the bank?"

"No, Sir."

"Right." Boyle wiped his face with his handkerchief and slumped into his chair. He stared at the debris in front of him. After a minute of what appeared to Fisher to be deep contemplation he looked up. "You're going to have a little holiday." Fisher looked concerned.

"A holiday?"

"Yes. When we go to Ireland next week you'll be staying there to look after my investment." Fisher's mouth became dry.

"For how long?" he said tentatively.

"For as long as I god dam say, that's how long!"

"Yes, Sir."

"You will report back to me everything that goes on, clear?" Boyle put away his sodden handkerchief. Fisher looked stunned. Northern Ireland was probably the last place on earth he wanted to go let alone to join a known terrorist group. "Am I clear?!" Boyle shouted as he slammed his fist down on the desk. Fisher was startled back to attention.

"Yes, Sir, quite clear."

"Good, now get out and shut the door." As Fisher left the room Boyle looked at his watch, picked up the telephone and began to dial.

Liam Donnelly was in bed and snoring loudly when the telephone rang. Waking with a start, he fumbled for the lamp, peering at the red LED digits of the clock as he lifted the receiver "Who is this?"

"Liam, it's Donald." Boyles' voice was stern and without apology.

"Donald? It's three thirty in the morning."

"Never mind that. I'm making a change to our arrangement." Donnelly sat up.

"What do you mean? What sort of change?"

"I'm bringing one of my men to join you." There was a pause as Donnelly considered. "Why would you want to do that, don't you trust me, Donald?"

"Let's just say I want to safeguard my investment." There was another longer pause then Boyle continued. "This isn't up for negotiation. You take my man or I keep my money." Boyle's voice was hard and unequivocal.

"Who is it?"

"Fisher"

"The lawyer! You must be joking?" Donnelly had met Fisher when he had visited Boyle and had instantly disliked him.

"That's the deal."

"You leave me no choice, I'll take your man, Donald, but I can't guarantee his safety. He'll stand out around here like a nun in a knocking shop."

"Not my problem. It's up to you to look after him. I'll see you on Monday." The line went dead in Donnelly's ear. Replacing the receiver, he took a cigarette and lit it and turning off the lamp, stared coldly into the dark.

It was 4pm on Saturday 17th. Two days had passed and Michael Prentiss felt that he was as ready as he could be. He had spent hours with Sergeant Jordan, Captain Noble and the lovely Lieutenant Preston, or Katie as he now knew her. He had tried to avoid the earnest little chats Dr Alexander wanted to have with him. Although they were supposed to be helpful Prentiss found dwelling on the ramifications of the operation unsettling. There would be plenty of time for counselling and therapy afterwards if he thought it necessary. For the moment however he just wanted to concentrate on the job in hand.

The time had finally arrived for his final briefing before departure. Prentiss sat in front of Colonel Mabbitt and Captain Noble in the classroom that now had all the familiarity of home. He knew he had changed over the past few days relishing every aspect of the training. His mind had become attuned to the environment in which he now found himself. He was focused, confident yet calm and relaxed.

"You have come a long way, my boy." Mabbitt said reviewing Prentiss' file. He looked up and smiled. "How do you feel?"

"I'm okay."

"Good." Mabbitt looked for any indications that Prentiss wasn't but there were none. "You will be leaving here in about an hour with Captain Noble and flying by helicopter to a remote location outside Londonderry. There you will transfer to a waiting taxi which will take you to the university. The taxi driver will of course be one of our people." Prentiss nodded. He had been over this many times.

"Once at the university you will be met by this man" Mabbitt continued, pointing to the photograph on the blackboard. "Professor Neil Barrington, who is your contact at the university and will get you into the Halls of Residence. From then on it's up to you to get yourself and a group of students into The Anchor on both Sunday and Monday night."

"Understood."

"Remember, you only need to take the gun on Monday for the operation. There is no sense risking the possibility of it being discovered on the reconnaissance the night before." Mabbitt had the tone of a concerned parent.

"Any problems, contact me on the agreed telephone number." Noble added. "As your handler I'll be your lifeline to the outside world."

"Once you've done the job we will be ready to extract you from the RUC whilst en route to the police station so be ready." Mabbitt continued.

"And the RUC won't have any idea of who I am?"

"No it's vital that we keep as few people in the loop as possible. We can't risk the possibility of someone in the RUC giving you away. It's not unheard of for police officers to be pressurised or blackmailed for information." Noble said. There was a silence. Each going over the operation in their head trying to think of some aspect of it that had been overlooked.

Finally Colonel Mabbitt spoke. "There's one more thing, Michael. As you know this is a strictly unofficial operation. If things go wrong you won't be able to contact the police or the army. Be assured we will get you out but until we do you will be on your own. Is that clear?" Prentiss nodded. "Right, you go and draw your equipment with Captain Noble then come and see me before you go."

Along the hallway Noble showed Prentiss into a small room. Jordan was going through the equipment that was laid out on a table. He looked up as the two men entered. "Right, Michael, this is everything you'll need for the operation. From now on you are Francois DuPont, French foreign exchange student. Here is your passport and Student's Union card." He handed Prentiss the documents. Opening the passport, Prentiss scowled at the photograph and commented.

"Christ, I wouldn't trust him."

Jordan smiled "Well you are supposed to be French." He then turned to an open suitcase. "Here we have one suitcase full of assorted tasteless clothes, all with French labels, toiletries, again all French. It's little details like this that can save your life although we've decided against the string of onions, stripy jersey and beret. Then of course we have a rather fetching pair of boxer shorts." He held up the adapted shorts in which Prentiss would hide the gun. "Now if you look here you'll see that there is a false compartment in the bottom of the case which is where your Beretta is concealed." Jordan slid back a panel to reveal the small automatic Prentiss had spent so many hours training with.

"Loaded?" Prentiss queried.

"Yes, I've given you hollow point ammunition. Not exactly legal but it'll give you an edge, absolutely devastating. One bullet per target will be all that you'll need but remember go for a head shot, they may be wearing body armour."

Prentiss nodded "understood."

"Finally here's two hundred pounds in cash, try not to spend it all. The drinks are on you when you get back." Prentiss gave a wry smile. "Well that's it. I know we got off to a bad start but you've learnt a lot. Trust your instincts and come back in one piece. Good luck, Michael" Jordan held out his hand.

"I'll see you Tuesday." Prentiss reassured as he shook his instructor's hand. Jordan smiled and left.

"Let's get all this stuff together and then I'll take you back to the Colonel." Noble said once they were alone.

Ten minutes later Prentiss was sat in an armchair in a small comfortable office on the top floor of Repton Manor. Opposite him Colonel Mabbitt poured two glasses of whiskey from a rectangular crystal decanter, handed one to Prentiss and sat down. Captain

Noble left the room. "Good man, Jeremy." Mabbitt said looking over at the closed door. "One of the best analytical brains I've ever known in this game. Did a stint in MI5 before coming back to me. He has a great deal of perspective; you'll be alright with him watching your back. Here's to Operation Ares." Mabbitt took a big gulp and savoured the whiskey. "That's better." He paused for a moment. "What do you know about Ares, Michael?"

"Not much. Greek God of War, wasn't he?" Prentiss replied putting down his glass. He was sure that the whiskey was a fine one but the pure malt was lost on him. He would have much preferred a lager.

"Zeus was the ruler of all the Gods on Mount Olympus. His Queen was Hera and together they had a son, Ares. Ares was not only, as you quite rightly say, the God of War but also of courage and civil order. He was brave and fearless and wore a suit of golden armour and carried a spear of bronze."

"And I'm your Ares, am I? But instead of a spear and golden armour I've got a gun in a pair of pants." Prentiss said dryly. Mabbitt smiled weakly then he became solemn.

"Just over a year ago the Shadow Northern Ireland Secretary, Airey Neave, was killed by a car bomb as he left the Houses of Parliament. They struck right at the heart of democracy. The bomb used was on a timer with a trembler so any movement would set it off. At that time not all vehicles were checked fully as they entered the car park as they are now so the police had no idea when or where it had been planted. Margaret Thatcher described him as one of freedom's warriors; courageous, staunch and true." Mabbitt leant forward "You are my freedom's warrior, Michael. It's time to strike back at these forces of evil."

Prentiss picked up his glass "Here's to freedom."

Mabbitt raised his. "Good luck, my boy."

Chapter Seven

The Gazelle touched down just before nine on Saturday evening in a field fifteen miles south west of Londonderry. Prentiss and Noble climbed out. Bending forward as they ran to avoid the rotor blades of the helicopter, the two shadowy figures headed towards a waiting MK.1 Cortina. Prentiss handed his suitcase to the driver's outstretched hand and turned to Noble. The wind was freshening from the north and thick clouds obscured any trace of moonlight.

"Good luck, Michael. Any problems, you know how to contact me."

"Will do."

"I'll see you on Monday once you've been extracted." Noble held out his hand and Prentiss shook it. "Remember, Michael, and this is important, trust no-one and stay in character no matter what. You mustn't let your guard down, not for a second. You are Francois Dupont, understand?"

"Yeah." He got into the taxi and it drove off into the darkness towards the lights of Londonderry.

Forty minutes later the taxi came to a halt outside the Magee campus halls of residence. The campus was named after the college that was originally founded in 1845 by Martha Magee. The widow of a Presbyterian minister, she inherited a fortune from her two military brothers to endow a college for the education of Presbyterian ministers. Situated just a short walk along the River Foyle, it stands away from the city walls having become an integral part of the University of Ulster in 1970.

The driver took the suitcase from the boot and, placing it on the ground, drove away without speaking. As Prentiss picked it up a thin wiry man appeared, his shock of long grey hair blowing uncontrollably in the wind. A bony hand at the end of a battered tweed sleeve was already outstretched and coming towards him like a lance. "*Francois Dupont*? Erm *Bienvenue bonsoir* erm *a l'universite de Magee.*" It was clear that this man couldn't speak a word of French and that this was a rehearsed welcome.

"Professor Barrington?" Prentiss asked in a thick French accent shaking the outstretched hand.

"Erm *oui Je suis* erm." Barrington flustered. Prentiss decided to put the professor out of his misery.

"Thank you for your kind welcome Professor but I would prefer to speak English while I am here." Barrington looked relieved and the fixed smile became relaxed and genuine.

"Splendid. Let me to show you to your room. Have you had a good journey from, Marseilles wasn't it?" Barrington ushered Prentiss into the building.

"Yes, very good thank you."

"Which university do you attend?"

"*Ze Paul Cezanne.*"

"Ah, the Head of Economics here studied at the *Universite de la Mediterranee*. I must introduce you to him. He lived in Marseilles for years."

"That would be very good," replied Prentiss thinking that this was someone he really did need to stay away from due to the, not so insignificant, fact that he had never been to Marseilles in his life.

A few minutes later Prentiss found himself in his room having thanked and said goodnight to the good Professor. The room was small but functional with a bed, wardrobe, desk and chair. Pulling the curtains he pushed the suitcase under the bed and looked at his watch. Ensuring the suitcase was secured with a large combination padlock, Prentiss left the room and headed for the student's union bar.

Following the sound of the music he entered the main building. It was 10.30 on a Saturday night and there were students everywhere. Prentiss walked into the bar. It was warm and noisy; laughter filled the large room. Isolated clouds of cigarette smoke hung above groups of students as they sat around tables chatting and giggling and flirting.

Prentiss scanned the room as he moved slowly from the doorway to the bar. After buying a lager he stood with his back to the bar. He looked across at the alcove to his left and found what he was looking for. Four male students, all aged about twenty, were laughing loudly, clearly the worse for drink judging by the large number of glasses that littered the table they surrounded.

"You'll do nicely" Prentiss muttered to himself as he took his drink and walked over.

By eleven o'clock Francois Dupont was a welcome and accepted member of the group.

Thirty minutes earlier a stolen blue Morris 1100 was heading out of Londonderry on the A6 towards Belfast. It contained two of Donnelly's gang. Behind the wheel was Lurgan-born Seamus O'Malley, with his greasy black hair touching his shoulders and matching handlebar moustache. A truly nasty piece of work, he bore the knife mark on his throat from his altercation with Donnelly earlier that week and was still seething from it. Next to him was Davey Duggan. His round face was permanently ruddy and, with his brown curly hair, he had the appearance of a farm hand. Although not a stupid man, he found independent thought a bit of a trial. Leant against his leg in the foot well was an Armalite rifle. Agitated, he looked over his shoulder out of the rear window to make sure that they weren't being followed. "I'm not sure about this, Seamus."

"Just relax will you?"

"But I don't think Liam is going to like it."

"Bollocks to Liam." Seamus hissed. "We've been sat around for weeks and I've had enough." His eyes were fixed on the road ahead of him, his knuckles white as he gripped the steering wheel.

"But Liam said we weren't to..."

"I don't want another word about Liam bloody Donnelly, do you hear me? This American shite is clouding his judgement." Seamus interrupted looking away from the road and staring at Davey intently with hatred in his eyes. Davey shuffled nervously in his seat saying nothing.

Ten minutes later they approached the intersection of the A6 and the A29 just outside Maghera. Seamus' dark eyes focused on the vehicle that was parked, just off the road on the opposite side to them, near the crossroads. The vehicle had no lights on so it was difficult to make out what it was in the dark until they were almost level with it. Seamus slowed gently to about thirty-five as they drove past the army Land Rover, casually looking at it as they continued down the road. The two Paras inside barely gave the blue 1100 a second glance as they were pouring tea from a Thermos flask.

Turning right at the crossroads away from Maghera, Seamus drove a quarter of a mile down the A29 and pulled over. The road was quiet with only an occasional passing car.

"Right, Davey boy let's get us a couple of Brits." Pulling on a black balaclava he reached into the back, grabbed a rifle and got out of the car. Reluctantly Davey did the same. The two men jumped the fence that enclosed the field and made their way back to the parked Land Rover.

Crouching as they ran, they approached the army vehicle from the rear. They were now only fifty yards away. Kneeling down Seamus could just make out something moving at the back of the Land Rover. A passing car's headlights on the A6 momentarily lit just enough for him to make out the figure of one of the soldiers.

"Good," he whispered "he's taking a leak, now's our chance." Pulling his flick knife from his jacket pocket Seamus began to move silently closer and closer to the unsuspecting soldier. Davey hesitantly followed behind him. Seamus was almost there. Ten more paces and he would be on him. The five inch stiletto blade glinted in his gloved hand. His breathing was heavy and muffled through the balaclava. Nine paces, eight, seven, then behind him Davey stumbled noisily. The soldier turned and shouted but Seamus was on him. Clamping his left hand over the soldier's mouth he thrust the knife deep into his victim's throat pushing him back against the vehicle. With the alarm raised the second soldier was already out of the Land Rover, pistol in hand. Davey clambered to his feet and raised his rifle. The paratrooper fired three shots in quick succession that thudded into Davey's chest. Leaving his knife in the dead soldier's throat, Seamus crouched behind the Land Rover as the body fell to the ground. Taking up his rifle, he broke cover. Still crouching, he fired up at the soldier who stood little more than five feet away. Instinctively, the paratrooper fired his pistol hitting Seamus in the upper right arm. A dozen bullets from Seamus' automatic rifle riddled the upper body of his second victim. He was dead before he hit the ground.

A car drove past. The driver looked but didn't slow down. He knew better than that. Seamus knew that he would have to move fast if he was going to escape the inevitable blanket of army and police that would descend on the area. Wincing as the bullet wound in his arm burned, he dropped the rifle. He was already starting to lose the feeling in his right hand as he pressed his left over the wound to try and stop the bleeding. The pain made him cry out. He could feel the warm blood trickling down his arm inside his sleeve. Seamus walked back to his first victim and retrieved his knife. He then turned and ran back to the car to make good his escape, pausing only briefly to look down at Davey's lifeless body.

Three hours later Liam Donnelly had been woken and aggressively questioned by the RUC Special Branch regarding the terrorist incident earlier that night. Having been aware of Donnelly's activities for some time they were constantly frustrated by the lack of any concrete evidence with which they could arrest him. Repeatedly they had asked him what he knew about his barman's, one Davey Duggan, part in the murder of two British army soldiers and who else was involved. After an hour of relentless and brutal questioning, Donnelly, having a cast iron alibi and denying all knowledge of the incident, watched the police leave with their customary threats and warnings.

Donnelly now sat in The Anchor bar with one of his thugs. He stared at his glass of whiskey deep in thought. The rage inside him that one of his men had flouted his specific order to take no action was burning like a flame. He knew that Davey was too stupid to come up with this on his own and considered who would get him involved? Finally his eyes narrowed "Seamus fucking O'Malley" he spat under his breath. He looked at his man behind the bar. "Get the van, we're going visiting."

Just after 4am on Sunday the rusty white Ford Transit van

pulled up outside the small two bedroomed terraced house in Lurgan. Donnelly got out of the van. It was still dark. He looked up and down the deserted street and then at the white painted house in front of him. He shoulder charged the wooden front door. It yielded instantly, splintering the door frame. He walked into the long narrow hallway followed by his man. With the door closed behind them Donnelly switched on the light. The house was still. Ahead of him was a staircase, the banister smeared with blood. The two men slowly climbed the stairs and turned the corner onto the landing. More blood, this time on the bedroom door handle. Donnelly pushed open the door and flicked on the light. Seamus lay on the bed; a large red blood stain was stark against the white bedspread. His hair was matted with sweat and his skin pallid and grey. Donnelly walked over and looked down at him. Seamus looked up at him with the eyes of a wounded animal. "It looks like the bullet has caught the artery, so it does." Donnelly said matter of factly looking at the bullet wound.

"Help me, Liam." Seamus pleaded weakly. "I'm bleeding to death."

Donnelly raised his eyebrows. "Oh that you are, Seamus, that you are. Very nasty."

"I need a hospital."

"You see what happens when you don't do as you're told? You get shot, poor Davey gets killed and I get a visit from the police in the middle of the night asking me all sorts of impertinent questions." He tutted and shook his head. "Davey was a good man, as thick as a brick, but a good man. We need good men, Seamus." Donnelly grabbed him by his shirt and pulled him up until their faces were only inches apart. "When are you people going to realise that this is war? A war that I intend to win. Not by killing a couple of British soldiers but by mounting a considered... strategic... campaign." He shook Seamus to emphasise his last three words then threw him back onto the bed.

"I'm sorry, Liam" Seamus writhed in agony. Donnelly leant forward and looked into Seamus' eyes. Picking up a pillow he pressed it over the injured man's face, took out his gun and fired two muffled shots into it. Showing no emotion, Donnelly put away his gun, took one last look at the body of the traitorous Seamus and, with a look of utter contempt, left.

Prentiss was woken suddenly the following morning by three sharp raps on his door. He squinted at his watch, 10.30. His head was pounding. The knock on the door came again, louder this time, reverberating in his head. "Just a minute." he called stumbling out of bed and crossing to the door. Opening it just a few inches he peered out. Prentiss' eyes widened with recognition but had the presence of mind not to say anything.

"Can I come in?" dressed casually in jeans and sweatshirt and sporting a woollen red beret was Katie Preston. Her blue eyes twinkled.

"What are you doing here?" Prentiss whispered pulling her inside. After checking the empty corridor he closed the door.

Preston pulled off her beret and sat down on the bed.

"Calm down and relax." She looked at Prentiss and smiled. He was suddenly aware that he was wearing only his underwear and a T-shirt so hurriedly pulled on his jeans.

"Is there a problem?" he asked as he dressed.

"Not exactly but Captain Noble sent me with a message. You won't be able to do your reconnaissance tonight."

"Why, what's happened?"

"One of Donnelly's men was involved in an incident last night. Two soldiers were murdered and he was found dead at the scene. Pretty gruesome by all accounts. Anyway, Donnelly has closed the pub for twenty four hours, a mark of respect I expect." Prentiss pulled up the chair and sat down.

"The operation's still on though, yes?"

"Yes. Your orders are to sit tight here until tomorrow and then to proceed as planned." Prentiss ran his fingers through his hair.

"Right." he replied. Preston could see that this change of plan had unsettled him a little so she thought she had better focus his mind.

"How's the integration going, looking at the state of you this morning, quite well I'd say?" She smiled her gorgeous smile. Prentiss sat back in his chair and blew out his cheeks.

"Fine, I've found four lads that are almost certainly majoring in hard drinking. I seem to have fitted in okay. Apparently I have a certain foreign mystery." He said in his French accent. "I'm meeting up with them again this afternoon."

"Good. Just hang around the campus and maintain a low profile until you go tomorrow night." She looked into his eyes. "Everything okay?" She allowed a hint of concern into her voice.

"Everything's fine." Prentiss reassured. Preston stood and pulled on her beret.

"I'd better be going; I'm based at Aldergrove for the duration of the operation." She kissed Prentiss lightly on the cheek. "*Bonne chance.*" He opened the door and, after once again making sure the corridor was still clear, he nodded to Preston who slipped out of the room and was gone. Closing the door he turned and leant against it with his throbbing head.

"It's going to be a long couple of days" he muttered quietly.

Chapter Eight

At just before eleven o'clock on Monday morning Donald Boyle's private jet descended from a cloudless blue sky and landed at Belfast airport. Boyle had slept through much of the eleven hour flight waking only to noisily eat a huge meal of half a dozen chilli dogs and fries, incongruously washed down with a bottle of 1961 Chateau Lafite Rothschild.

As the plane taxied to a hangar away from the main terminal buildings Marcus Hook released his safety belt. Standing on the floor between his legs was the large leather attaché case containing half a million dollars in cash. Coming to a halt the plane's engines powered down as the co-pilot emerged from the cockpit. Opening the pressurised door he lowered the steps into place. Fisher was the first out of the plane to meet the waiting customs official and deal with the relevant documentation. Donald Boyle climbed down the steps breathing in deeply, closely followed by Hook carrying the case.

"Smell that air, Hook?" Boyle said "We're in the land of my forefathers." Hook made no response as they made their way to a waiting black Daimler limousine. The bodyguard stood by the car as Fisher supervised the loading of the luggage into the boot by the co-pilot.

"I'll take that." Hook barked as a small brown leather suitcase was about to be put into the boot with the rest of the luggage. Gripping it in his huge hand he got into the front passenger seat next to the driver. As always Fisher got into the back next to Boyle.

With the attaché case once again between Hook's feet he placed the small suitcase on his lap and opened it. He rummaged to the bottom and pulled the tab that lifted the floor of the case to reveal a false bottom. From it he took out his .45 automatic pistol in its holster. Having checked the weapon he flicked up the safety catch to the on position, put it back into the holster and slid it onto his belt under his jacket.

In the back of the Daimler Boyle had noticed how quiet Fisher had been. "What's the matter, boy? You've barely said a word since we left the states."

"I wish you would reconsider your decision to leave me here. I mean, these people are terrorists." Fisher replied.

"Don't be so pathetic." Boyle scorned "I need somebody here to look after my interests and that somebody is you. What do you think I pay you for?"

"I'd like to be alive to spend it."

"Just do as you're told." There was no compassion or even humanity in Boyle's voice. Fisher remained in silent contemplation for the rest of the journey as to how much he loathed and despised Donald Boyle.

Forty-five minutes later, having driven west, the Daimler glided through the fifteen acres of beautiful secluded grounds and woodland of the Shamrock Hotel. As Fisher checked them in Boyle stood in the lobby admiring the many original paintings by Joseph Carey and Robert Gregory that covered the walls. Hook stood no more than five feet away from Boyle. He scanned every face and movement in the busy hotel lobby. His eyes flashed as two porters chatting to a pretty blonde chambermaid emerged from one of the wall of elevators to his right. Examining them briefly and deciding that they were no threat his eyes moved to the young couple looking at the tourist information literature, again no threat. His attention then turned to a middle aged man sitting in an armchair drinking coffee and reading a newspaper. He stared at him intently for a moment. Just as he considered him a threat, a flustered woman of a similar age appeared, full of apologies. The man gave a long suffering smile, put down his paper and the couple left. No threat. At that point Fisher arrived with the hotel manager to accompany them to Boyle's suite.

As the elevator doors closed the pretty blonde chambermaid stood in a secluded corner of the lobby. Lieutenant Preston took out a walkie talkie from the pile of towels she was carrying, held it to her lips and whispered. "The target has arrived."

In the communications centre at RAF Aldergrove a Royal Signals corporal pulled off her headset and called over to Captain Noble. "Excuse me, Sir. We've just had confirmation of the target's arrival at the Shamrock Hotel."

"Excellent." Noble said with a thin smile and, turning on his heel, he made his way to his office. On entering he stopped suddenly in the doorway expecting the office to be empty.

"Ah hello, Jeremy there you are."

"Colonel, I thought you were remaining at Ashford?"

"Yes I was but I decided to monitor things from here. Not that I haven't got the utmost confidence in your ability to run the operation, Jeremy." Mabbitt returned a file to his briefcase and sat behind the desk.

"Thank you, Sir."

"So where are we?" Noble closed the door and stood in front of his commanding officer.

"Preston has reported that Boyle has arrived at the hotel."

"What about The Anchor?"

"Intelligence reports that it's reopening this evening."

"Good. Strange business that. Why would Donnelly murder two servicemen on the eve of such an important deal?" Mabbitt paused. "It doesn't make sense."

"I suspect, Sir, that it was carried out without Donnelly's approval. The RUC found another of Donnelly's gang members, Seamus O'Malley's body at his home this morning. He had been shot twice in the head." Mabbitt nodded as he listened.

"Retribution for daring to improvise." The Colonel said.

"Yes, Sir."

"Is Michael set?"

"Preston reported that everything was in place and he was ready to go."

"Right, I'm off for some lunch. Keep me apprised of any developments." Mabbitt gathered his things and patting Noble on the shoulder, stalked out of the office.

In The Anchor, Liam Donnelly stood before what was left of his gang. There was a nervous silence in the room. His making an example of Seamus O'Malley had certainly had the deSired effect on the rest of his men. Donnelly sat down and spread his fingers out in front of him on the table, his arms outstretched.

"You will have heard the sad news about Seamus," he said, staring at his hands. "The result of acting on his own initiative." He looked up at the faces of each his men. Donnelly's voice was cold and controlled. "I trust there won't be any repetition of such...... independent thought?" The gang shuffled uncomfortably. Donnelly clapped his hands loudly. "Right then, the man coming here tonight is called Donald Boyle. He is an American. With him he will be bringing the cash that will fund the next step in the war against the British. He'll also have his assistant, Thomas Fisher, with him. He will be joining us."

"Can we trust him?" one of the men asked.

"I don't see why not, but watch him all the same. They'll arrive here at eight o'clock. I want you all to make sure that nothing goes wrong. Keep your eyes and ears open from the minute we open, right?" The assembled group nodded. "Okay, meet back here at six-thirty." They all got up to leave. As they did so Donnelly spoke to the man nearest to him. "Finton, hang on just a minute."

"Yes, boss." The young man in his early twenties sat down again.

"I want you to contact this man." Donnelly handed him a piece of paper. Finton looked at it with a puzzled expression.

"Who is it?"

"An arms dealer based in Hamburg, that's his name and phone number. I want you to call him, tell him you speak for me and that you want to arrange delivery of the items I ordered."

"Okay but why do you want me to do it?" he queried.

Donnelly drew closer conspiratorially "I'm pretty sure that I'm being watched." Finton nodded. "He'll want to know that you work for me so tell him, the coffee our mutual friend had with him in Munich was too strong for his taste. Use those exact words. He'll understand. Make sure you do it from a call box just in case the phones are tapped."

"I will, Liam." Donnelly gripped the young man's forearm and pulled him closer.

"I'm trusting you with this, Finton, don't let me down."

"I won't, Liam." Donnelly released him.

"Good lad, away with you now." Finton stuffed the piece of paper into his jacket pocket and hurried away.

Thirty minutes later Finton was standing in a phone box dialling the long international number to Hamburg. As it rang he went over in his mind his rehearsed speech. Finally the phone was answered. "Yes?" The voice spoke in English but with a thick German accent. Finton gathered himself.

"Is that Kurt Schroeder?" There was silence then the voice came again.

"Who is this?"

"I'm speaking on behalf of Liam Donnelly."

"How do I know that?"

"The coffee you had with your mutual friend in Munich was too strong for him." Again there was silence. "Herr Schroeder?"

"I am Schroeder. Where is Donnelly? Why hasn't he contacted me himself?" The voice was slow, deliberate.

"He thought it was safer this way." Finton replied looking around him. "He wants to arrange delivery."

"There's a disused airfield near a place called Ardboe, Cookstown. 10pm tomorrow. Have my money ready." Before Finton could reply the line went dead. Finton smiled to himself, Liam would be pleased with him he thought as he quickly walked back to The Anchor to report.

Michael Prentiss loathed inactivity. He had always felt that he had an extremely low boredom threshold. He had coped reasonably well yesterday, having spent most of the day and evening with his drinking gang. Today however was different. It was Monday. His four mates all had lectures and, of course, he did not. He was forced to lie low in his room and stay out of sight to avoid any awkward questions. It was also the day of the operation. He tried to remain focused on the job in hand. This was the first real period of time he had spent not learning, practising, remembering or assimilating large amounts of information. Floor plans, street maps, telephone numbers and codes were all locked into his head for this one day and he was now struggling with the frustration of waiting.

Prentiss exercised intensely during the afternoon, partly to pass the time but primarily to get his endorphins pumping before finally collapsing on the bed. He slept fitfully for a couple of hours then woke with a start. He looked at his watch, five-thirty, due to meet the lads in an hour. It was time to prepare. He pulled his suitcase from under the bed, unlocked it and took out the modified boxer shorts that had caused so much amusement at Ashford. Having pulled them on, Prentiss opened the false bottom in his suitcase to reveal the hidden compartment that contained his Beretta. He took it out and held the gun. It felt reassuringly familiar in an unfamiliar environment. Removing the magazine Prentiss confirmed that it was fully loaded then re-inserted it, pulled back the slide and flicked the safety backwards to the 'on' position. He looked at the gun for a moment then slid it into the pouch. It was held firmly just above the pelvic bone, the barrel pointing towards the left thigh at forty-five degrees.

Prentiss quickly finished dressing, checking himself in the mirror to make sure that nothing showed. He gathered up his passport, student ID and the remainder of his cash. Putting on his black leather jacket he took one last look at the room before heading off to meet his drinking friends.

As Prentiss walked into the student's union bar a few minutes later he caught sight of a familiar mop of ginger hair propping up the bar. Steve Corrigan, unimaginatively nicknamed

'Ginger' was the first of the four to arrive.

"Hello, *mon ami*" Prentiss said tapping Ginger on the shoulder and greeting him with a warm smile.

"Francois!" Ginger exploded "How's it going?"

"I am very well *merci*." During the previous couple of days Prentiss had perfected the art of speaking English with a French accent while throwing in the odd word of French for good measure. Ginger looked over Prentiss' shoulder and exploded again

"Mikey!" A tall gangly figure nodded as he walked towards them.

"Alright, lads. What about you?" Mikey said throwing his arms round Prentiss and Ginger. "The other two bastards not here yet?"

"Who are you calling bastards!?" yelled a voice from the door. Two large rugby player types stood in the doorway looking furious at Mikey for a moment then throwing their heads back and roaring with laughter. Donal and Gerry joined the three at the bar. "Frankie!" Gerry said slapping Prentiss hard on the back "Bon bloody jour, my old frog's leg."

"Ah, Gerry you stupid Irish how do you say…spud. Are you ready for a night on the town?" Prentiss asked. He had become genuinely friendly with the four students. They were all from Northern Ireland and found their new 'foreign' mate with his quirky sense of humour entertaining.

"So where are we going?" Ginger asked.

"I have been told about a pub that is not too far from here where the girls are, 'ow you say, top 'eavy." Prentiss nudged Gerry in the ribs smiling and nodding. Gerry's eyes widened with excitement.

"Well it sounds absolutely bloody perfect. What's it called?"

Prentiss replied with a broad grin. "The Anchor."

Chapter Nine

It was just after seven-thirty by the time Prentiss and the four students neared The Anchor. The constant banter faded into the background as Prentiss focused on the pub. Seeing the Victorian building for the first time dried his mouth. He was filled with a combination of excitement and fear, mostly excitement which he put down to adrenalin. Prentiss looked at his hands, his palms were sweating. He knew if he was going to abort the operation now was the time, but there was no question of him doing that.

Two doormen stood by the entrance watching the group approach through the car park. Prentiss took a deep breath as one of the men held up his hand. "Just a routine search, lads." he said placing himself between the door and the group. Ginger grumbled something under his breath and held his arms out to the sides. Gerry did the same as the two doormen began the body search.

"Is this a traditional custom here?" Prentiss joked. One of the doormen looked at him briefly before continuing the search.

"It's just a security thing," replied Gerry over his shoulder. "You'll have to forgive our friend, he's French," he jovially said to the doorman.

"You can go inside," he replied flatly. "You, froggy" Prentiss took Gerry's place in front of the humourless individual.

"Bonjour" Prentiss said as his search began. The doorman's hands were large and carried out the search with a considerable degree of expertise. Having checked Prentiss' upper body and arms he concentrated on his legs, his hand passing briefly over Prentiss'

crotch.

"You can go in." He said finally.

"*Merci*" Prentiss smiled and with that he was inside.

He stood just inside the door and waited for the others. This gave him an opportunity to orientate himself. He had memorised the floor plan at Ashford and so it all looked strangely familiar. Prentiss was standing on the edge of a large open space. There was dark wood everywhere from the uncarpeted floorboards to the bar on his left that ran some hundred feet, almost the length of the room. Although still quite early the bar was busy and raucous laughter came from everywhere. Gerry, Donal, Mikey and Ginger were now gathered around Prentiss and the five of them made their way to the bar. Prentiss glanced at his watch, seven forty-five. He leant on his forearms against the bar and ordered a round of drinks. Casually he scanned the bar but there was no sign of Donnelly or Boyle and his party. All he could do now was to wait.

After ten minutes the air was filled with the sound of Irish folk music as a band began playing. Standing on a small foot high stage in the farthest corner of the pub, the band comprising of two fiddles, a flute and a guitar received rapturous cheers as the locals all raised their glasses in salute. As Prentiss watched, out of the corner of his eye he glimpsed a familiar figure emerging from a door behind the bar. He felt the hairs prickle on the back of his neck as he recognised Liam Donnelly. Taking a drink, Prentiss watched over his glass as Donnelly made his way through the crowd to the front door. He stood in the doorway for a few moments then greeted his visitor with a handshake and a vigorous slap on the shoulder. With Donnelly leading the way Prentiss saw his target for the first time. Close behind him was Marcus Hook followed by Thomas Fisher, who carried the attaché case. Prentiss watched as the four men walked to a table set apart from the others close to the stage. He quietly blew out his cheeks. The photographs of Hook really didn't do him justice. The man had menace emanating from every pore and Prentiss decided that he would be staying as far away from him as possible until nine-thirty.

Prentiss positioned himself so that he could watch the four men over the shoulders of Mikey and Ginger. He studied Boyle from his vantage point at the bar. The man was pouring with sweat and constantly needed to wipe his forehead with a large white handkerchief. He was wearing a dreadfully gaudy blue and white flowered short sleeved shirt, the front of which shook violently when the man laughed. When he wasn't laughing he was breathing hard, typical of someone so grossly overweight. This was in complete contrast to his two companions. Fisher could barely raise a smile and looked pale and tired. He looked about him constantly and reacted nervously to any sudden or unexpected movements. Clearly, thought Prentiss, this was not a happy man. Hook looked at Fisher from time to time with disdain as he would an obnoxious child. He disliked fear in anyone, regarding it as weakness. Leaning over he whispered something in Fisher's ear then continued to scan the room uninterested in the reaction his comment had caused. Fisher took a large swallow of whiskey and remained silent. Donnelly, on the other hand, was doing most of the talking. Prentiss focused on him and realised that, although the big Irishman laughed and was quite the jovial host with the American, his eyes remained cold and predatory. The more he studied the man's eyes the more he was reminded of those of a shark, dark and expressionless. This was a man who enjoyed his violent life and Prentiss knew that he wasn't going to stop until somebody stopped him.

By eight forty-five the pub was full with drinkers and a cloud of cigarette smoke hung heavily in the air. Ginger and Donal were busy chatting up a couple of local girls while Mikey and Gerry were trying to make an impression on a third by each extolling their own virtues over the other. Prentiss stood at the bar and watched his friend's antics.

"Are you not joining in?" A soft Irish voice said from behind him. He turned and saw a girl of about twenty looking at him with the most gorgeous green eyes. He gazed at her for a moment and then realised she was talking about his friends. He briefly looked at them over his shoulder and replied, "Not really my type."

"What accent is that, French?" She smiled and tucked her long red hair behind her ear.

"*Oui*, er yes" Prentiss replied in character. "I am studying at the university here for a while. Are you a student?"

"No I'm a nurse at the Altnagelvin. It's a hospital in the city."

"I'll know where to come when I feel *malade*."

"I just love the French accent, it's so romantic." She put her empty glass on the bar. Prentiss noticed a small silver cross hanging on a chain round her neck.

"That is very beautiful" he said pointing to it

"Thank you, my Grandmother gave it to me when I was little. She is very religious. She always says, I myself do nothing. The Holy Spirit accomplishes all through me."

"William Blake." Prentiss said recognising the quotation. The girl looked pleasantly surprised.

"Yes, that's right. He's her favourite poet."

"May I buy you a drink?"

"*Merci Monsieur*, I'll have a Bloody Mary."

"*Bon,* What can I call you?"

"My name's Orla." Prentiss found the girl captivating. She had a small beautiful face and a smile that he found enchanting.

"It's a pleasure to meet you, Orla. I'm Francois." Prentiss smiled and, as he ordered the drinks, looked over to Donnelly's table. He realised that he had been so completely distracted by this lovely girl he hadn't been watching his target. Boyle was looking distinctly the worse for wear. Clearly the large quantity of Irish whiskey with which Donnelly was plying him was having more than the deSired affect of making him feel relaxed. Boyle leant forward and said something to Donnelly slapping him on the forearm as he did so. Prentiss tried to focus on the men's conversation without Orla noticing. Boyle was attempting to stand whilst Donnelly was laughing and holding onto his arm. Hook stood and began to help Boyle to his feet. The fat American took Donnelly's hand and shook it.

Prentiss swore under his breath as he realised that Boyle was preparing to leave. He looked at his watch, eight fifty-three. Over half an hour before the RUC was due to arrive. He knew that he would have to think of something and quickly if he wasn't going to be forced to scrub the operation. His mind was racing. There must be something he could do. Then an idea began to form but he had no time to think it through. He was just going to have to go with it and hope for the best.

"Would you excuse me for just a moment?" he said to Orla. "I need to go to the bathroom."

"Okay," Orla replied but Prentiss was already moving down the bar towards Boyle. In different circumstances nothing would have dragged him away from getting to know this girl better but now he had to concentrate. Making his way through the crowd, he picked up a half empty bottle of Coca Cola from one of the tables. Boyle, followed by Hook, was leaving their table and heading for the door. Prentiss was now approaching some ten feet in front of him. He began to stagger and sway as if drunk and stumbled into Boyle spilling most of the remainder of the Coca Cola down Boyle's shirt. Instantly Hook grabbed Prentiss by the throat and gripped him tightly.

"*Pardon Monsieur.*" Prentiss gasped as Hook's huge hand compressed his windpipe.

"It's okay, Hook. Let him go." Boyle said wiping the drink off his shirt with his handkerchief. Obediently Hook released Prentiss who massaged his stinging throat as he gathered himself.

"I am so sorry *Monsieur*. It was an accident." Prentiss began wiping Boyle's shirt with his hand while maintaining eye contact. "You are American?"

"Yeah I'm an American." Boyle replied drunkenly as he looked at Prentiss' muscular frame.

"I like Americans; they are so big and strong." Prentiss squeezed Boyle's shoulder through his sweat-sodden shirt. He had remembered Boyle's proclivity for young men and decided to use it. "If you will excuse me, I was on my way to the bathroom." Prentiss said holding his eye contact with Boyle as he eased past him. He could feel Boyle watching him as he made his way to the door marked 'Toilets'. Prentiss hoped that he had done enough to whet Boyle's disgusting appetite and entice him to follow.

As Prentiss got to the door the band came to the end of another of their folk songs and the bar erupted with cheers and applause. The smiley red-faced guitarist wearing a cap and a threadbare waistcoat stepped forward and, inviting Liam Donnelly to the stage, held out a Bodhran. Donnelly mounted the stage, took the Irish drum from the guitarist and held it aloft triumphantly to the crowd. More cheers followed as the band began another song.

Prentiss stepped through the door and looked back to see if he had held Boyle's interest. He had. Prentiss smiled briefly at the sweating American and closed the door. He now found himself in a corridor that ran the width of the back of the building behind the stage. The shabby white paint on the brick walls was peeling and there were tiles missing from the quarry-tiled floor. Prentiss leant with his back to the door for a moment. Immediately to his left was a door marked 'Fire Exit'. Fifteen feet to his right were the two doors of the toilets. He walked down the corridor pushing open the first door on his left and went into the men's lavatories.

The rest room was twenty feet long with cubicles on the left wall, wash hand basins opposite and half a dozen filthy urinals at the far end. From one of the cubicles the toilet flushed and an elderly man emerged. Aware that Prentiss was there, he avoided looking at him. He just put his hands in his pockets and shuffled away without speaking. Prentiss checked the cubicles in turn, they were all empty. Satisfied that he was alone, he placed the plastic Cola bottle on the ledge just above his head in front of him as he took up position at one of the urinals, his back to the door.

It wasn't long before the door swung open briefly amplifying the music from the band before it closed again. Prentiss tried to control his breathing as he felt his heart begin to pound in his chest. He looked over his shoulder. There stood Boyle with Hook behind him. Boyle stared at Prentiss as Hook pushed open each of the cubicle doors. Having made sure there was no one else present he nodded to Boyle.

"Wait outside." Boyle ordered. Hook glared at Prentiss for a moment then did as he was told. Prentiss turned and faced Boyle who swayed from side to side. Boyle wiped the saliva from his mouth with the back of his hand as he drooled with anticipation. You really are a repulsive individual, thought Prentiss as he reached up for the bottle on the ledge and took a provocative sip. Boyle's heavy drunken eyes widened at this. He started to undo his trouser belt. Prentiss did the same taking a couple of steps forward as he did so Standing less than ten feet apart, Prentiss unbuttoned his jeans and slowly lowered the zip.

"Would you like to see what I've got here for you, *Monsieur*?" Prentiss asked playfully as he put his hand inside his shorts. Boyle watched Prentiss' hand with feverish excitement.

"Have you got something in there for me?" slurred Boyle.

"Oh yes" replied Prentiss quietly. He pulled out the Beretta. In one fluid movement he flicked off the safety, held the bottle over the end of the barrel as a make-shift silencer and fired. The smile fell from Boyle's face as the gun coughed once. There was a flash and a spray of blood and bone as Boyle fell backwards. He lay dead on the floor on what remained of the back of his skull.

Prentiss breathed hard and steadied himself on one of the hand basins. He looked down at Boyle's body. The bullet had entered just above the left eye and a large pool of red blood was forming on the filthy white tiled floor beneath him. He fought back the urge to vomit. He had to focus. Hook was just the other side of the door in the corridor ensuring that Boyle would not be interrupted. Prentiss did up his jeans and, stepping over the body, he listened at the door. He could hear voices; American voices.

Outside in the corridor Fisher had entered from the bar still carrying the attaché case. Hook's eyes darted towards the bar door as he came through it but relaxed slightly when he recognized Fisher.

"What is it?" snapped Hook stepping away from the door and moving towards him.

"You gotta help me; I'm desperate. I can't stay here with these…" he paused stumbling for the right word before spitting out "people."

"You've got no choice." Hook sneered. "Just get a hold of yourself and grow some balls." He turned to resume his position outside the toilet door but Fisher grabbed his arm. Hook spun back and threw Fisher against the wall and held him there. With his face only inches from Fisher's, Hook was unaware of the toilet door opening very slowly. Prentiss peered through the gap. Hook was standing eight feet away with his back to the door. This was his chance. Wrapping his leather jacket around the gun in his hand to muffle the sound, he stepped into the corridor. Fisher became aware of movement out of the corner of his eye as Prentiss raised his gun.

"No!" Fisher screamed. Hook looked, following Fisher's gaze as Prentiss fired twice hitting Hook between the shoulder blades. Arching his back, Hook began to turn, his right hand reaching for the holster at his hip beneath his jacket. Prentiss fired again hitting Hook in the mouth, propelling him backwards on top of Fisher. Removing the gun from his jacket, he pointed it at Fisher as he moved closer. Hook lay still, his lifeless eyes stared up at

Prentiss. Beneath him lay a terrified Fisher repeating the word "No" over and over, convinced he was about to share Hook's fate.

"Please," he begged, "take this" he pushed the attaché case towards Prentiss. "There's half a million dollars in there. It's yours just don't kill me." Prentiss looked at him. Killing Fisher was never part of the operation. Knowing that he could be discovered at any time, he pulled on his jacket and picked up the case. Taking the money with him would ensure that Donnelly wouldn't get his hands on it. He pushed open the fire exit door and was gone.

Once outside Prentiss ran to the rear of the building and, tossing the case over first, he climbed the boundary wall and dropped into the street that backed onto the pub. It was dark and fortunately the street was empty. He looked at his watch, five past nine. Prentiss knew that he had better lay low for a while as far away from the pub as possible. It wouldn't be long before the entire area was crawling with police and army patrols. Stuffing the Beretta in his waistband he started running down the dimly lit street. He had done it. Not only successfully completed his mission but had got the money as well. All he had to do now was get home. When it was safe he'd find a phone box and arrange for an alternative extraction. For the moment though he just had to keep running.

Chapter Ten

It was twenty past nine when the door to Colonel Mabbitt's office flew open and an uncharacteristically flustered Captain Noble burst in. Having sprinted up two flights of stairs from the communications room he was now standing in the doorway breathing hard.

"We have a problem. There are reports of a terrorist incident at The Anchor in Londonderry. Two Americans shot dead."

"What?" Mabbitt looked at his watch. "Where did we get this information?"

"Routine monitoring of the RUC police band. I was in the comms room preparing to put our anonymous call in." Noble rubbed his chin nervously and looked at his commanding officer. "Prentiss?"

"Oh yes, it's Prentiss alright. Has to be. My God, he's actually done it. Question is, what's he up to?" replied Mabbitt slowly. "Do we know where he is now?" Noble shook his head.

"Police reports say the gunman fled the scene, current whereabouts unknown. RUC are setting up checkpoints and distributing a partial description."

"So he's out there on his own, at least for the time being. If he keeps his head he'll go to ground then find a way of contacting us for an extraction." Mabbitt shook his head. "What went wrong?"

"Do you think he panicked?"

"I don't know, my instinct says not. More likely he's been

forced to be creative," he replied distantly. "Be ready, Jeremy; we've got to bring that young man in safely."

"Yes, Sir" Noble turned to leave.

"Oh and Jeremy, ask Katie to come and see me when she has a minute."

In Londonderry, Michael Prentiss was now a mile and a half away from The Anchor having used only the side roads and back alleys to avoid the increasing numbers of roving RUC and army patrols. He knew that he couldn't risk emerging onto the main roads as anyone remotely matching his description was being stopped and questioned at gunpoint. He sat down with his back against a brick wall in an unlit alleyway behind a row of terraced houses. He had no idea where he was as he had been forced to constantly change direction almost stumbling on police checkpoints on more than one occasion.

Suddenly he heard the familiar sound of an army Land Rover driving up the street at the end of the alley. Pulling the collar of his jacket up over his cheeks, Prentiss pressed himself against the wall and turned his face away. The army vehicle drove slowly past without stopping. Prentiss grabbed the attaché case and ran to the end of the alley. Cautiously he peered into the street and watched the Land Rover turn left at the junction and disappear from sight. As it did so he focused his attention on the phone box that was illuminated by a street light some twenty feet from the junction Good, Prentiss thought. Now I just need somewhere quiet to hide for a while. Prentiss studied a building site across the road secured by a ten feet high dilapidated green corrugated iron fence. One of the panels had been vandalised and pushed in at the bottom creating a small gap large enough to crawl through. That'll do, thought Prentiss as he ran across the road towards the fence daubed with the loyalist graffiti that had become so commonplace on the streets of Londonderry.

Having squeezed himself through the gap in the unforgiving corrugated iron panels, Prentiss waited for his eyes to adjust to the darkness. Without the street lights the ground in front of him was eerie and unsettling. He began to make out the unfamiliar shapes of the piles of earth, rubble and twisted metal that were all that now remained of what once had been a factory. He had no idea that this was where the body of Sergeant McMullan had been discovered earlier that month. It began to rain hard, a cold soaking rain that made Prentiss shiver. He picked his way cautiously over the debris slipping as he did so as the rain turned the ground to a muddy wasteland. Just ahead of him amongst the rubble he saw a section of concrete sewer pipe. He reached it and looked inside. The pipe was four feet in diameter and six feet long and although the bottom of it was littered with broken bricks and masonry at least it was dry.

Clambering inside Prentiss pulled the case in behind him. Still shivering he looked around in the near darkness for something to wrap around him. He found nothing. If there was anything he couldn't see it in the gloom, so, using it as insulation against the ground, he sat on the case and pulled his knees up to his chest. Prentiss looked at his watch. The luminous dial glowed brightly; ten-thirty. He decided to wait until three. It should be quiet enough to make contact then. He wrapped his arms round his legs, put his forehead on his knees and tried to sleep.

At RAF Aldergrove Captain Noble sat uneasily in his office. He had left orders in the communications room to be alerted as soon as there was any information about Prentiss but as yet there was no word. The murder of the highly respected American oil tycoon, Donald Boyle, and his 'associate' was all over the news. Nobody had claimed responsibility for the shooting in the Londonderry pub but the police were actively seeking Francois Dupont, a French exchange student at the University of Ulster, who had gone missing since the incident.

It was a little after midnight and Noble sat back in his chair and rubbed his eyes. It had been a long day and there was no sign of it ending any time soon. The silence of his office was broken by the telephone ringing. Noble had two telephones on his desk. Green, which received all internal calls and outside calls via the switchboard, and Cream, that was a direct line outside. Picking up the cream receiver he answered with his name.

Instantly he recognised the voice. "What the hell are you doing ringing me here?" he whispered in a mixture of anger and panic.

"You just be quiet, Jerry m'boy, and listen. You and me had

an arrangement, so we did. You wouldn't be trying to double-cross me would you?"

"What are you talking about?"

"Your wee soldier, that's what I'm talking about!"

"He did the job didn't he?" Noble's voice hardened.

"Oh, yes. He did it alright. Quite a neat little job as a matter of fact."

"So what's the problem?"

"The problem, Jerry boy, is that your man has made off with my bloody money!" Noble fell silent.

"Christ almighty," he murmured finally.

"So, Jeremy, if I find out that you have decided to alter our arrangement you won't live to see the sun come up."

"Of course I haven't" Noble replied angrily. "It's that little shit improvising and not sticking to the plan. Don't worry I'll deal with it when he contacts me to bring him in."

"I'm not worried. Just make sure you do." The voice was slow and menacing.

"And just remember" Noble sneered "It's *our* money, not *yours*; half of it belongs to me. I'm not doing this for some idealistic cause; I just want to be rich. I'll be in touch." He replaced the receiver. In a call box in Londonderry Liam Donnelly stood stone faced as he watched the rain beat hard against the glass.

By two-thirty on Tuesday morning Noble had heard nothing from Prentiss. He dozed uncomfortably in his chair when the telephone rang and woke him with a start. He reached for the cream phone hoping it was Prentiss but realised it was the green internal phone that was ringing. Answering it he heard Mabbitt's voice asking him to "pop up for a minute." Reluctant to leave his direct line for any longer than was necessary, Noble quickly made his way to the CO's office, knocked once and entered.

"Yes, Sir?" he asked closing the door. Mabbitt looked puzzled.

"I've been summoned to Gower Street." The Colonel announced. Hearing the address Noble sat in the chair in front of Mabbitt's desk.

"Why? What do MI5 want at this time of night?"

"They didn't say."

"Operation Ares?"

"Bit of a coincidence if it isn't, wouldn't you say? What troubles me is how did they find out about it?" Mabbitt looked intently at Noble. "Any thoughts?" Noble shuffled uncomfortably in his chair shaking his head.

"No, Sir." Mabbitt rose from his chair and Noble respectfully did the same.

"Oh well, I was just wondering. I know that you still have your contact at 'five' from your time with them. What was his name?"

"Peter Collins."

"Ah yes."

"Who are you seeing?" Noble asked.

"Sixth floor." Mabbitt replied raising his eyebrows. Noble

knew that the Director General's office was located on the sixth floor. "I'm flying out in ten minutes. Keep on top of things here while I'm gone. Jeremy, it's vital that we get Prentiss back or this could all turn very ugly, clear?"

"Clear, Sir." Noble left Mabbitt's office and made his way back to his own. As he did so Noble allowed himself a little smile. With Mabbitt out of the way he now had a free hand to resolve this intolerable situation without the unwelcome oversight of that wily old sod.

As Colonel Mabbitt's helicopter took off from Aldergrove bound for London, Michael Prentiss woke suddenly in his hideout. His sleep had been filled with the recurring images of Donald Boyle and Marcus Hook's violent last moments. He tried to move but the cold and inactivity had left his limbs stiff so he stretched, as best he could within the confines of the pipe, to get some feeling back into his legs. The luminous dial on his watch read two forty-five. Time to make a move, he thought, and he crawled out of the sewer pipe. Deciding that he would be less conspicuous if he left the case where it was, he concealed it under a pile of bricks. He stood up straight and stretched once more, rubbing each thigh in turn to increase the circulation. Prentiss took the Beretta from his waistband and secured it in the compartment in his shorts considering that he was less likely to be shot if challenged if they thought he was unarmed.

The rain had stopped but there was now a strong, cold wind

blowing. Prentiss started picking his way back to the opening in the fence. His jeans were wet and clung uncomfortably to his legs while his feet were soaked, having stumbled into the many deep puddles in the darkness. He just had to focus on that hot bath that was waiting for him at Aldergrove. Emerging from the building site, he crouched on the pavement as he looked up and down the street. There was nobody there. Crossing the road, Prentiss ran towards the telephone box watching the main road ahead of him for any movement. Within seconds he was inside the phone box and dialling. It rang a couple of times in his ear and then he heard a familiar voice. Having pushed in the two ten pence coins, Prentiss spoke calmly "XNY 556 A for Ares request immediate extraction." In his office in Aldergrove Captain Noble closed his eyes momentarily with relief.

"Good to hear your voice, Ares. Give me your location."

"I'm not sure - can't see any street names. I passed a church earlier, Saint Augustine's I think. I can make it back there." Noble searched the street map of Londonderry on his wall.

"Saint Augustine's. Got it. It's on Palace Street. We can be there in thirty minutes. Can you get there okay?"

"Don't worry I'll get there."

"Are you still armed?"

"Yes."

"Good. Look for a brown Granada. Two of my people will bring you in."

"Got it."

"Well done, Ares. We'll soon have you home," Noble said reassuringly.

"I'd better go." Prentiss hung up and ran back towards the alley to retrace his steps to the extraction point. Even before Prentiss had reached the alley Noble's bony finger was dialling. Donnelly lifted the receiver without speaking. Noble was brief and succinct.

"Saint Augustine's Church, Palace Street, thirty minutes. Be careful, he's still armed." He hurriedly hung up. Noble sat back in his chair and took a deep breath then let it out slowly. He knew it was now just a question of keeping calm and waiting.

Ten minutes later a knock came at Noble's door and Katie Preston appeared with news that wiped the smugness off his face.

"Excuse me, Sir I've just come from 'comms'. The RUC have picked up someone matching Prentiss' description." Her face was flushed as she delivered the news.

"What! When was this?" Noble asked, visibly shaken.

"About five minutes ago. We are continuing to monitor the police band for further information but it doesn't look good, does it, Sir?" Noble didn't reply he simply gripped the arms of his chair. "Sir?" Preston asked "What are we going to do?" Before Noble could answer the green telephone rang. He leapt on it

As he listened silently Preston could see the panic drain from the captain's face and be replaced by an expression of calm relief. "Thank you." he said replacing the receiver. "That was 'comms,' the suspect they arrested was some petty burglar trying to break into a newsagent's."

"Thank God. So he's still out there somewhere. Do you think he's okay?"

"For the moment we have to assume that he is. I'm sure he'll contact us when he can," reassured Noble. "All we can do is wait for his call. Don't worry, Lieutenant; he's a resourceful young man. We'll get him back." Preston tried to look reassured and returned to 'comms.' Noble looked at his watch, fifteen more minutes.

Prentiss had made good time and he was nearing Saint Augustine's church. He approached the church scanning the road ahead for movement. He reached the gate. No brown Granada, just a number of parked cars and an old Ford Transit all of which were empty. Prentiss felt exposed standing on the pavement so he slipped through the gate and into the churchyard. The wind blew the trees hard, bending their branches with its force. He took up position in the churchyard, crouching behind a large headstone that afforded him a good view of the road. Prentiss looked up at the church behind him. Neo-Gothic in style, the whinstone and sandstone building had been here for over a hundred years and stood on the site of a former monastery dating back to 546 AD.

Prentiss looked at his watch, three, thirty-five. They should have been here by now. He began to feel uneasy. As he tried to decide what to do if Noble's men didn't show he heard the growing sound of an engine getting nearer. "About bloody time," he muttered and looked around the headstone, immediately pulling back as an army patrol drove by. Too close, he thought as he pressed his face against the cold wet stone. Prentiss crouched motionless and listened as the engine grew fainter and fainter. The knot in his stomach tightened. He was so nearly there, just a few more minutes and safety. Allowing his mind to wander, he thought about Colonel Mabbitt, Captain Noble, Sergeant Jordan and, of course, the lovely Katie. How proud they would be of him for what he had achieved. Where the hell was that bloody Granada? Prentiss looked at his watch again. Three forty-two. As he began to feel that something had gone wrong he felt a searing pain in the back of his head and everything went black.

Chapter Eleven

It was a bright sunny morning as Colonel Mabbitt entered MI5 headquarters at 140 Gower Street, in Bloomsbury, London at six-thirty precisely. Having quickly cleared security he was escorted to the sixth floor in the lift but, instead of being led into the Director General's office as he expected, he was shown into a conference room at the end of the corridor. A large round table was set for a meeting of twelve but only two of the chairs were occupied.

As he entered a familiar face stood and extended his hand. Mabbitt shook it. "Good morning, Charles." Mabbitt briefly detected the merest hint of a smile from his host.

"Morning, Dominic, you're looking well," Mabbitt replied. He threw his overcoat on the back of an empty chair. He was feeling tired and irritable and really wasn't in the mood for this man this morning. Widely known in the service as 'the little snide', Dominic Fellows was the Head of the Northern Ireland Section. The product of Eton and Cambridge, he had been recruited into MI5 whilst reading Classics at university. Now at thirty-three he had run the Northern Ireland Section for almost a year. Fellows didn't plan on remaining as head of section for long. His sights were set firmly on the DG's office and he didn't care who he had to step on to get there. Considering himself superior in almost every way to his contemporaries, he disliked most and distrusted all.

Fellows now found himself facing a man with whom he had

almost nothing in common. Charles Mabbitt had built a successful career using his courage, instinct and experience, never being afraid to take risks to achieve the deSired outcome. Dominic Fellows, however, believed in playing it safe. He had a reputation for covering his own behind, often at the expense of those around him. He knew how to use people to get things done. Ingratiating himself with superiors, he was always ready to take the credit for success and distance himself from failure.

Fellows tugged at the cuff of his hand-made shirt revealing two inches of crisp white linen and a flash of gold cuff link beneath the sleeve of his navy pinstripe Savile Row suit. "Charles, may I introduce Brad Mason from the CIA? Brad, this is Colonel Charles Mabbitt, commanding officer of the Fourteenth Intelligence Company." Mason stood and shook Mabbitt's hand with a vice-like grip. At six feet five he stood head and shoulders above both men. The introductions dealt with, all three took their seats.

"Tea, coffee?" Fellows asked.

"No thank you, Dominic, I'm a little pressed for time so I would appreciate it if you would move speedily to the point and tell me why you wanted to see me. I'm rather busy at present."

"Yes, of course. That would be the unsanctioned covert operation you currently have under way in Londonderry." Mabbitt stared at him impassively. "You don't deny that you have mounted an unauthorised operation that has resulted in the violent deaths of two US citizens?" The supercilious tone in Fellows voice reinforced Mabbitt's opinion of the man that he really was a waste of organs. "You see" Fellows continued, relishing every moment, "I assured Brad here that you would have a sound explanation as to why a senior intelligence officer would countenance such an operation." Fellows sat back in his chair and interlaced his fingers, resting them on his stomach.

"Yes, Dominic, I'm sure you did,"

"And the explanation is?" The two men looked into each others eyes with mutual contempt.

"I received intelligence that Donald Boyle was prepared to fund Liam Donnelly, a target we currently have under surveillance, in a new campaign both in the province and here on the mainland. The first deposit of half a million dollars was brought by Boyle in cash and delivered to Donnelly in person last night in Londonderry. I considered this to be a credible threat to the security of this country."

"You considered." Fellows repeated.

"Yes."

"I see."

"Left unchecked we would have been faced with a level of terrorist funding, from Boyle and then others following suit in the United States, that would herald unparalleled terrorist activity on a scale we have never seen."

"If it was such a credible threat as you say why didn't you put in for Home Office approval?"

"Because I wouldn't have got it," Mabbitt replied calmly.

"So you took it upon yourself to murder this man."

"Yes."

Fellows spluttered incredulously "My God, Charles, your arrogance is blinding! Your mandate is to gather intelligence on terrorist activity in Northern Ireland, not to assume the role of contract killer."

"I did what needed to be done to ensure the safety of this country."

"And in doing so have ruined a joint MI5, CIA operation that, coincidentally, did have official approval."

Mabbitt's eyes narrowed. "I am not aware of such an operation"

"Well perhaps it was considered a little above your pay grade and more prudent to exclude you from this one."

"Considered prudent by who? You?" Fellows didn't reply, merely raised an eyebrow. Mabbitt resisted the urge to bury his fist into Fellows' smug round face and continued. "It is my unit that is tasked with intelligence gathering in Northern Ireland and as such I am to be included in all intelligence matters to avoid any overlap or duplication of operations."

"This was too important to be handled by... someone like you." Mabbitt leapt to his feet at Fellows' sneering comment and leaned across the table, barely able to control his anger.

"Donald Boyle...!"

"Donald Boyle was a CIA asset!" Fellows shouted. Mabbitt fell silent and looked at Mason, stunned at the revelation.

"It's true, Colonel." The American said softly. "Please, sit down." Mabbitt resumed his seat and Mason continued. "Dominic came to me, obviously with the same intelligence that you had. When it became clear what he was doing, Dominic asked us to lean on Boyle with a view to coercing him into working with us. To be honest it wasn't terribly difficult to do with his, how shall we put it, colourful lifestyle. We gave him photographs we had acquired of a young man's dead body that Boyle had strangled when one of his sex games went too far."

"I'm sorry but I'm not following this. What did you want Boyle to do?"

"Simple" answered Fellows "We wanted Boyle to put a man into Donnelly's cell ostensibly to safeguard his investment but in reality a source to relay intelligence back to Boyle and in turn to us on all terrorist activity. Something I believe you've been trying to do for a while Charles with rather lamentable success."

"Thomas Fisher." Mabbitt concluded.

"Yes, Charles, Thomas Fisher. But thanks to you and your mischievous little unit we now have no pipeline into Donnelly's cell and a terrorist sitting on half a million dollars in cash."

"Fisher flew out of Belfast in Boyle's private jet an hour ago and is high tailing it back to the States as we speak," Mason said.

"Well, Charles, it's all a bit of mess, isn't it?" Fellows said brightly. "And to make matters worse I understand that your man has gone missing, whereabouts unknown." Mabbitt didn't reply clearly deep in thought. Brad Mason stood and buttoned his jacket.

"Well I'd better be getting along and leave you guys to it."

"Thanks, Brad I'm really sorry it has ended like this. We must keep in touch." Fellows shook his hand vigorously with an apologetic 'none of this is my fault' expression.

"You guys should start talking to each other. After all, you're both supposed to be on the same side." He took Mabbitt's hand firmly and while shaking it said "Pleasure to meet you, Charles; I hope you get your man back."

"We're working on it."

"I hope Charles hasn't permanently soured our relationship, Brad." Fellows' obsequiousness was just too much for the CIA man to stomach.

"If you'll take a tip from me, Dominic; this whole situation could have been avoided if you had concentrated on the job rather than point scoring to further your own career. To be honest with you, I think you're an asshole. I'll see myself out." He nodded respectfully to Mabbitt and left.

Fellows stood with a doleful expression, embarrassed at the American's rebuke.

Mabbitt smirked for a moment then saw Fellows' eyes flash. "You won't find it very amusing when I press for an official enquiry into this fiasco. You are aware of course that the PM is due to have her secret visit to Northern Ireland this week?"

"I am."

"Can you imagine if word reached her delicate shell-like ears that you are autonomously operating some kind of a death squad over there, targeting innocent Americans? I guarantee you won't be looking so bloody smug then."

"I agree the timing is…unfortunate. Nevertheless…"

"Nevertheless a great deal of planning has gone into this visit tomorrow and nobody but nobody is going to muck it up. Am I clear?"

"Oh yes, Dominic. Crystal." Mabbitt picked up his overcoat and turned to leave. "As a matter of interest, Dominic, where did your intelligence come from, that Boyle wanted to fund Donnelly?"

"Not that it's any of your concern but it came from one of my junior desk officer's informants. Why?"

"Do you remember his name, the desk officer?"

"Yes, it was Collins in Belfast but why the interest?"

"Just curious. Thank you, Dominic, I'll be in touch." Mabbitt swept out of the office.

"Don't think this is over, Charles because it's not. Not by a long way!" Fellows shouted after him but Mabbitt was already at the lift and heading for his waiting car.

In Londonderry an hour earlier Michael Prentiss was suddenly roused from unconsciousness as a set of plastic Venetian blinds were loudly pulled up and the early morning sun shone into his face. A voice boomed close to his ear "Wakey wakey, rise and shine" as a hand grabbed his hair pulling his head back. Disorientated and unable to see, Prentiss tried to raise his hands to shield his eyes from the light. He found that both of his arms were restrained, secured in some way to each of the back legs of his chair. The pain coming from the back of his head generated an overwhelming wave of nausea causing him to vomit uncontrollably into his lap.

"Jesus Christ!" laughed the voice from behind him as the hand released Prentiss' hair, allowing his head to fall forward once again. The vomiting stopped, leaving him coughing and gasping for air.

With his head still pounding Prentiss' eyes began to focus; first on the stinking mess on his shirt and jeans, then on his surroundings. He was in a domestic kitchen not dissimilar to that in his family home in Grantham. The walls were painted a canary yellow, blue linoleum covered the floor and against the far wall was a Formica topped kitchen table. He was sat on a wooden kitchen chair. Although his arms were restrained at the wrists by what felt like gaffer tape, his legs remained free.

Standing in front of the window by the sink was a thin man in his early twenties. His hand rested on the butt of an automatic pistol stuffed into his waistband. Prentiss squinted in the sunlight. He was aware of movement behind him. Slowly a large figure walked round the chair and Liam Donnelly looked Prentiss in the face. "I don't think we've been introduced, Liam Donnelly's the name. What's yours?" He bent forward until his face was just a few inches from Prentiss' and then recoiled "My god you stink." he chortled. "Finton, clean him up." Finton turned and filled a bucket with water from the tap and threw it over Prentiss. "That's better." said Donnelly cheerfully pulling up a chair and sitting in front of the dripping Prentiss. "Now then, what's your name?" Prentiss stared at him. "No?" Donnelly opened what Prentiss recognized as his passport. "According to this you are Francois Dupont and this tells me that you are a student at the university." Having read the student's union card he flicked it at Prentiss.

"Well, Francois Dupont, the first thing you need to know is that nobody is coming to help you because nobody knows that you're here. The second thing is that you can make as much noise as you like and nobody will hear you. You are completely alone, understand?" Prentiss decided that he would remain silent for as long as he could. He knew that Mabbitt and the others would be doing all they could to find him.

"You were very impressive last night. I didn't spot you until you made your move, and I knew that you were coming. My god what a mess, they'll be cleaning up for weeks. I thought that Donald only smelled bad on the outside." He laughed. "As for that bodyguard of his. I take my hat off to you, so I do. He was a big bastard, bloody scary if you ask me. Still, they'll be no loss, certainly not to me. What I want to know is this. Where is the money you took last night? You didn't have it with you when you were picked up which means that you've hidden it, you cunning wee frog." Donnelly's voice hardened. "So where is it?" Prentiss said nothing; just stared in defiance.

"Oh, feeling brave, are we? Well we'll see about that." Donnelly slowly began to roll up his shirt sleeves. "Now, some people in my line of work like to use pharmaceuticals, you know, drugs and that, to extract information. Some people use intimidation, tell me what I want to know or I'll kill your family, that type of thing. But me, I'm what you might call a traditionalist." Donnelly stood. "I like to use pain." He punched Prentiss hard on the cheekbone knocking him and the chair backwards. Prentiss felt the right chair leg give a little. Finton pulled Prentiss and the chair upright and stood holding it from behind.

"You see it not only brings results but I do find it rather satisfying." He punched again this time in the stomach leaving Prentiss winded and fighting for breath.

"Where's the money?" The back of Donnelly's fist struck Prentiss hard on the temple sending a jarring pain through his head and blurring his vision. "Where is it?" Prentiss shook his head remaining silent. He was punched again, then again. He hadn't undergone any anti-interrogation training and so didn't have any of the techniques to help him resist Donnelly. Although no amount of training could have prepared him for the relentless pounding. As the attack continued his mind drifted to all the war films he had seen where the British officer had been captured and interrogated by the Gestapo. The only thing the prisoner said was 'I have nothing to say.' Prentiss decided to be that British officer. Over and over in his mind he repeated I have nothing to say, I have nothing to say, until finally he passed out.

Five minutes later another bucket of water brought Prentiss

back. His face was numb and didn't feel as if it belonged to him any more. Donnelly was pacing, getting more and more frustrated with Prentiss' silence. Finton looked worried.

"What happens if you can't make him talk, the delivery is set for ten o'clock tonight? If you don't have the money…"

"Don't worry, he'll talk." Seeing that Prentiss was conscious he stopped and faced him. "Tough little bastard, aren't you? But you will tell me where that money is. Trust me, everybody talks in the end." Donnelly picked up a brown canvas tool bag and banged it down on the table. He took out a power drill and an extension cable. Connecting the two, he grabbed a handful of drill bits. Examining them carefully he selected a thin spindly one and inserted it into the drill.

"Plug me in, Finton." Finton did as he was told. Donnelly pressed the trigger momentarily and the drill roared to life and then died away. "Good" he said to Prentiss, smiling then, putting the drill on the table, returned to the tool bag. After rummaging for a few seconds he produced a two inch rubber ball. He tossed it lightly into the air and turned to Prentiss.

"Last chance; tell me where the money is." Prentiss slowly shook his head. "No? I couldn't help noticing what lovely teeth you have there, Francois." Donnelly squeezed Prentiss' cheeks to look inside his mouth. "Yes, lovely teeth. That'll be because you're foreign I suppose. All that calcium in the cheese. I've never liked the dentist myself, something about the drill." His voice flattened, saying each word deliberately. "Where... is... the... money?"

Prentiss' fear subsided as he looked intently into Donnelly's eyes and was replaced by hatred.

"Right" said Donnelly as he began to put the rubber ball into Prentiss' mouth.

"Wait!" Prentiss said in his French accent. Donnelly stopped.

"That's better. I told you, Finton. Everyone talks in the end."

"You couldn't start with the one at the back could you? It's been giving me some trouble." Prentiss said. His defiance made Donnelly wild with fury.

"You're a funny wee frog, so you are." He seethed pushing the ball hard into Prentiss' left cheek. Picking up the drill Donnelly nodded to Finton. "Hold him." Finton grabbed Prentiss by the hair with both hands, pulling back his head. As Donnelly switched on the power drill Prentiss shut his eyes. This was going to be bad.

It had only been just over a minute but Prentiss could endure no more. Donnelly's drill had burrowed deep into the molar and then the gum at the back of his mouth. As it did so the tooth splintered sending fragments down his throat causing him to choke uncontrollably. Unable to breathe, Prentiss writhed in agony trying to scream but couldn't. Finally, Donnelly stopped and removed the ball while Finton let go of Prentiss' head allowing it to fall forward. Thick gloupy blood poured relentlessly from his mouth. Donnelly, breathing hard, threw down the drill and wiped the sweat from his forehead.

"Well? Where is it?" Before Prentiss could answer a telephone rang in another room. Donnelly looked at his watch. "I need to get that." He said to Finton "Clean him up." As he left the kitchen to answer the phone Finton crossed to the sink and began to fill the bucket.

Prentiss felt the top of the chair leg joint with his fingertips. It had loosened considerably during his torture and he hoped that if enough stress was applied to it, it would break. He looked at Finton who stood with his back to him. As Donnelly answered the phone himself Prentiss deduced that he, Finton and Donnelly must be alone in the house. This was likely to be his only opportunity to escape. He launched himself at Finton turning as he did so. The chair hit Finton square in the back with such force that he fell forward hitting his head on the taps. The loosened leg came away from the frame and fell to the floor freeing his right hand. With it still attached to his left, Prentiss lifted the chair and brought it crashing down on Finton's head submerging it in the almost filled bucket. Prentiss held the struggling man's head under the water. Frantically Finton tried to fight back but Prentiss' weight on the chair frame prevented him from raising his head. The muffled screams in the bucket gradually faded until Finton became limp and slumped lifeless to the floor.

Prentiss knew he didn't have long. Releasing himself from the chair he took the gun from Finton's waistband. As he did so the door flew open. Instinctively Prentiss fired twice from his crouched position on the floor. Both shots missed embedding themselves in the wall near Donnelly. He fired twice more, then again. It was the final shot that found its mark and hit Donnelly just below the clavicle near his right shoulder. The big man spun round with the impact of the bullet and fell down the wall into the corner.

Prentiss sat frozen, the gun still trained on Donnelly who lay motionless in a heap. Eventually Prentiss lowered the weapon. He was dazed and exhausted, driven mad by the pain in his mouth. The water, still pouring into the bucket in the sink, overflowed onto his shoulder bringing him sharply back to the stark reality of his situation. He stood and turned off the tap. Drops of red blood blobbed into the bucket. Washing as much of the blood from his face as he could he looked down at Finton. He searched the dead man's trouser pockets. Discarding the keys and a comb he took the wallet and threw it on to the table. He looked around the room. Slung on the back of a chair by the table was a green parka coat. He winced with pain as he put it on. Prentiss pulled his Beretta from its hidden compartment and stuffed it, his passport and union card together with Finton's gun and wallet into the pockets. He zipped up the coat and walked out of the kitchen stepping over Donnelly as he did so. Reaching the front door he pulled up the hood to conceal his battered swollen face and stepped out to freedom.

Chapter Twelve

It was eight-thirty on a Tuesday morning and Prentiss found himself on a large council estate. Groups of teenage uniformed school children walked down the road all heading in the same direction. This was not at all what he expected to find after the horror of what he had just endured. Prentiss found it all to be unnervingly normal. Having no idea where he was, he decided to follow and see where it led him.

Having walked for some five minutes he neared the edge of the estate. The houses gave way to more and more open space. He looked over to his right and below him he could see the city and the river. Prentiss approached an empty bus shelter. He was feeling weak and light headed. A sharp pain racked his torso as he moved and the drilled tooth and gum, although no longer bleeding, with the nerve now exposed was agony. Reaching the bus shelter, he slumped down on the seat. The ground inside was covered with long shards of broken glass where one of the windows had been smashed. Prentiss stared at the gable end of a house he had just passed. Painted on the wall almost twenty feet high was the black silhouette of an IRA soldier. Clearly a boundary marker he thought.

A couple of minutes later Prentiss saw a blue and white bus approach the estate obviously from the city. He squinted at the one word destination displayed on the panel above the windscreen, Creggan. "Oh shit, I'm on the bloody Creggan Estate" Prentiss muttered then winced as the cold morning air touched what was left of his tooth.

The Creggan Estate sits high on the West Bank of the city of Londonderry. Built shortly after the war, it was the first estate in Derry built with the sole purpose of housing Catholics. Located above the Bogside and almost on the border with Donegal, it is one of the most notorious housing estates in the whole of Northern Ireland. Prentiss suddenly felt very alone. He was an innocent in an unholy land and he longed for the safety of home. For the first time he didn't know what to do. He had gone over the events of the last few hours in his mind many times and two things didn't make sense. Why hadn't Noble's men turned up at the extraction point and how did Donnelly know where to find him? He didn't like the obvious conclusion. Someone at Aldergrove, maybe Noble himself, told Donnelly where to find him. Prentiss dismissed the idea that it could be Noble. Why would he? What would he have to gain? He had spent time with him, trusted him. No, it must be someone else, but who?

An army patrol approached from the city. Prentiss cradled his ribs with his arm and turned to examine the timetable printed on the back wall of the shelter until the Land Rover went by. His legs began to shake and he found it difficult to focus. The traffic was becoming more frequent now. Looking up the road he saw a handful of women with shopping bags heading towards the bus shelter. He knew it wasn't long before the bus would arrive on its return journey into Londonderry. If he could just hold on for a few more minutes he would be able to rest on the bus.

The shelter began to fill with women grumbling at the broken glass littering the ground and eyeing Prentiss with suspicion. He stood outside, leaning heavily against the shelter. Whispering loudly amongst themselves as they watched Prentiss, the women tried to decide whether the scruffy young man was a glue sniffer or on drugs. Prentiss, realising that he was drawing too much attention to himself, decided he had no alternative but to abandon the bus and get away from the inquisitive gaggle of women. Clutching his chest with his head down, he started to walk slowly towards the city. He hadn't gone more than twenty feet when the world spun round and he fell to the ground. In the distance he could hear the women venting their disgust at somebody so drunk that early in the morning.

While Prentiss lay on the ground dazed and in pain he became aware of a car stopping next to him and the driver getting out. "Are you okay?" The concerned voice was soft and feminine. She turned Prentiss over. "It's alright I'm a nurse." She looked at his beaten face. "My God, what's happened to you?" Then she looked closer. "Wait. I know you; you're that French guy from the pub last night, Francois." Prentiss recognized the girl looking down at him.

"Orla, help me," he said weakly. "Please." Orla nodded and helped Prentiss to his feet and into her blue mini, its engine still running.

"I'll take you to the hospital." She said once they were under way.

"No, you can't do that." Prentiss replied without his accent.

"You're no more French than I am. Who are you really?"

"You wouldn't believe me if I told you. Is there somewhere quiet we can go?"

"Not until you tell me who did this to you. Are you with the provos? Because if you are you can get out.." Prentiss tried to laugh at the irony but it hurt too much.

"No, I promise I'm not. Look, I'll tell you what I can but first I need somewhere to rest." Orla looked across at the exhausted Prentiss as he closed his eyes and decided that she would help him, for now.

Prentiss slept most of the journey to Orla's flat waking only briefly as she helped him inside and laid him on the bed. After thirty minutes he woke to find her gently dabbing his face with some cotton wool.

"Where are my things?" He asked, suddenly aware that he was naked under the sheet.

"Over there" Orla nodded to the pile of stinking clothes in the corner.

"Did you take them off?"

"I did, there's no way you were going to lay in my bed in those disgusting things."

"I see."

"Oh don't be such a big baby. You haven't got anything I haven't seen before."

"Where am I?"

"My flat, you're quite safe."

"Do you live here alone?"

"No, I have a flatmate, Suzy, but don't worry she's at work, which is where I should be. Now shut up while I do this." Obediently Prentiss lay quietly and looked around the bedroom. It was small but very neat. The walls were painted lavender and the bed was Victorian polished mahogany matching the wardrobe and dressing table. On the wall at the foot of the bed hung a large print of Van Gough's Sunflowers.

"So, who are you and don't give me some old flannel about being a student." Orla said sternly as she finished with his face.

"All I can tell you is my name is Michael and I'm in a bit of trouble."

"Trouble is it? I'll say you're in trouble. You've got a gash on the back of your head, probable concussion, a face that looks like it's been smacked with a shovel, not to mention a couple of cracked ribs and severe bruising."

"Actually I've also got a bit of toothache." Prentiss pulled the corner of his mouth open with his finger. Orla looked inside.

"My God, who did this to you?"

"Someone with a lot of questions and a rather large power drill." She left the bedroom returning a couple of minutes later with a bottle of Aspirin and a glass containing a drop of water.

"I'll mix up a paste to put on that but you really need to go to a hospital."

"I will but there's something I've got to do first." Orla began to crush the Aspirin into the glass and mix it with a spoon.

"They say you killed those two men in the pub last night. Did you?"

"Yes."

"So if you're not a terrorist what are you?"

"That's a good question; I only wish I had a good answer."

"Who were they anyway? The news said that they were innocent American businessmen on holiday."

"They were American businessmen alright but they were certainly neither innocent nor on holiday." There was a long silence.

"You're not going to tell me who you are, are you?"

"That wouldn't be my first choice, no. Look it's safer for you that you don't know too much about me. I'm in a country full of terrorists that take great delight in killing each other so the less you know the better." Orla's expression changed from concern to anger as she thrust the glass into Prentiss' hand.

"Here, put this on your tooth, or what's left of it and I hope it's agony." She stormed out of the room.

Orla got her wish. As Prentiss applied the paste to his gum and tooth it was indeed agony. So much so that he cried out, rolling around the bed. Gradually, the more he applied the more the pain subsided to a tolerable level. Orla appeared at the door.

"We're not all like that. There are a lot of good, decent people in the six counties. People that just want all the violence to stop. So they can live their lives just like everybody else without having to worry about a small but very powerful minority with their guns and their bombs and their misguided ideals. Yours is precisely the sort of prejudice that fuels a lot of the problems here. Your kind has no idea what it's like to live here. I've grown up with it. I've seen friends killed in the name of religion or nationalistic cause just for being in the wrong place at the wrong time. And you, you come here with all your guns and your preconceived ideas; you're no better than they are." Orla stood indignantly with her hands on her hips.

"I'm sorry; I've had rather a bad day. What I meant was there are people after me that would think nothing of killing you just for being seen with me. I don't want to be responsible for that. I feel bad enough getting you involved at all." Prentiss tried to smile. "Thank you for helping me. I don't know what I'd have done without you. Really, I'm not like them. I'm just in the middle of something …. complicated. So I'm asking you to trust me." Orla's face softened.

"So, I'll be trusting you, will I?" She looked at the battered figure in front of her. "What can I do to help?"

"I could do with some clothes."

"My flatmate's boyfriend stays over sometimes; he's about your size. You can borrow some of his things." Orla turned to fetch the clothes as Prentiss added.

"Have you got a phone?"

At RAF Aldergrove, Lieutenant Katie Preston sat in the

communication centre holding a cold cup of coffee. Her face was pale and her normally sparkling blue eyes were red with tiredness and worry. She had maintained a vigil in 'comms' all night, willing Prentiss to make contact and confirm he was okay. Of everyone in the unit she felt his disappearance the keenest. She had grown very fond of him during their time at Ashford feeling almost maternal to the inexperienced young man. She had uncharacteristically voiced her concern as to Prentiss' ability to successfully complete such an operation to the Colonel, only to be told that he was confident in his ability and not to worry. But now she was worried. It had been over twelve hours since Boyle and Hook had been shot and there was still no word from him.

The phone at her workstation rang and she answered immediately. It was an operator from the far side of the comms centre.

"Lieutenant, there's a call for you, it's your brother. He knows he isn't supposed to call you here but it is some kind of family emergency."

"Put him through." she said cautiously. There was a click in her ear as the call was transferred and then came Prentiss' voice.

"Katie, it's me, don't react or say my name. Is this call being monitored?"

"No we can talk. Are you okay?"

"I've been better."

"When you didn't check in we were beginning to fear the worst."

"What?"

"You've had us all really worried."

"Katie, I rang at three o'clock this morning for an extraction."

"I don't understand. I've been in comms all night nothing came in here."

"I didn't go through comms. Captain Noble gave me his direct line number while we were on the chopper over here. Are you telling me that he didn't tell you he arranged my extraction?"

"Michael, I'm telling you that there was no extraction." They both fell silent.

"Oh God, Katie. Noble's mixed up with Donnelly."

"Michael, you're jumping to conclusions. There must be some mistake."

"No, there's no mistake. It explains why Donnelly's thugs turned up instead of the extraction team. And something else has been bothering me. Donnelly told me that he knew I was coming last night. How would he know that unless someone in the unit had told him?"

"Do you know what you're saying?" Preston said incredulously.

"Look, Katie, I know I'm a bit tired and emotional as I've just spent the night helping Liam Donnelly perfect his DIY dentistry skills but someone is hanging me out to dry."

"Alright, alright I'm going to bring you in myself then we'll take this to the Colonel. Is Donnelly still after you?"

"No, he's dead. Him and one of his men."

"I see. Where are you?"

"Safe enough for now. There's one more thing. I took Boyle's money last night and hid it. We need to retrieve it before it's discovered."

"Okay, give me the details." As Preston listened to Prentiss she saw Noble walk into comms and begin talking to the duty officer. As she wrote down the location of the attaché case Noble began to make his way towards her. "Meet me there at twelve," she said, hurriedly replacing the receiver, ripping off the sheet from the pad and hiding it under the desk.

"Everything alright, Lieutenant?" Noble inquired.

"Fine." she replied innocently.

"Who was that you were talking to?" He looked at Preston with an intensity she found unsettling.

"Ballykelly, see if they had heard anything."

"You look tired, Lieutenant."

"I am. Would it be alright if I got a couple of hours sleep?"

"Good idea. I'll let you know the minute we hear anything." Preston screwed up the paper in her fist and picked up her bag.

"Thank you, Sir." As she left the comms centre Noble watched her with suspicion. He approached the duty officer again.

"I'd like to see this morning's phone logs."

"Yes, Sir." He handed Noble a computer printout. He studied it carefully until he saw what he was looking for.

"A call came in a few minutes ago from off-base and was put

through to Lieutenant Preston. Where did it come from?" The duty officer consulted the printout.

"Corporal Harris, the call for Lieutenant Preston at 09.47 what was its origin?"

"A personal call, Sir, from her brother. A family emergency."

"Thank you corporal." Noble said slowly. He knew the personnel files of his entire unit. Lieutenant Preston didn't have a brother.

Chapter Thirteen

Q cars were a fleet of anonymous looking saloons fitted with civilian number plates which were used by The Det when carrying out surveillance activities in Northern Ireland. Specially modified, these vehicles were Kevlar armour plated to protect the occupants. In the event of an ambush, gaps in the plating allowed the operators to fire their weapons through the bodywork and a multi 'flashbang' launcher secreted beneath the vehicle launched stun grenades in all directions before detonating. In addition a number of defence systems were in place to detect any tampering of the car's electronics indicating that a bomb had been planted. It was one of these Q cars that Lieutenant Preston had signed out from the car pool and was driving towards Londonderry.

It would take her just over an hour to cover the fifty or so miles from Aldergrove to the location Prentiss had given her. The beige Granada's two litre engine responded with a growl as she pressed her foot hard on the accelerator. With Noble thinking that she was sleeping in her quarters Preston had left the base discreetly, not telling anyone where she was going. She considered it safer that way. If Noble was a traitor he may not be working alone. With the Colonel on his way back from London and Sergeant Jordan still in Ashford, Preston knew that it was up to her alone to bring Prentiss in safely. Once she had done that she could take it all to Mabbitt for him to deal with.

At Orla's flat Prentiss was beginning to feel better. Now

dressed in some fresh clothes he was sitting at the kitchen table attempting to eat some scrambled eggs. Orla had insisted that he try in her bossy, matronly way but it was proving too painful with his lacerated gum and splintered tooth.

Finally he gave up. "I'll eat something when I've seen a dentist." He said pushing the plate away from him.

"How's your head?" Orla asked sipping coffee from the mug she cradled in both hands.

"Better."

Orla looked at Prentiss. "Can I ask you something?" she asked hesitantly.

"You can ask." Prentiss smiled.

"What did it feel like, killing those men last night?"

"It's hard to explain." Prentiss replied finally. "I suppose it felt like I was detached from the whole thing. A bit like a dream. It didn't exactly go according to plan and it was all over before I knew it. I've thought about it a lot since. I mean, these were really nasty people, Orla. What they were doing meant that there was no other choice."

"You think that they deserved to die?"

"I don't think anyone deserves to die. But it was necessary to prevent a lot more people from getting hurt. So if you're asking me whether I regret it, then the answer is no, I don't."

"What will you do now?"

"I'm afraid I need you to help me just once more."

"What do you need?"

"Do you have a street map of the city?" Orla crossed to a kitchen drawer and took out a tatty street map. Spreading it out on the table Prentiss studied it for a moment then pointed.

"Can you take me here?"

Orla looked. "Yes, no problem. It's about twenty minutes away."

"That's where I'm being picked up, and then I'll be out of your hair for good." He looked at his watch. "We'll leave in an hour."

Doctor Sean Hamilton was a man whose life had spiralled out of control. Publicly disgraced in the local press and struck off by the General Medical Council, his life, like his career, was in tatters. A once successful and respected surgeon, Hamilton had hidden, what began as a glass of whiskey to unwind at the end of the day, a bottle a day drink problem for almost two years. Needing three glasses to stop the shaking before he kissed his wife and children goodbye in the morning, it became increasingly difficult to conceal his alcoholism from his colleagues at the hospital. The secreted bottles in his office were visited more and more often just to get him through the day. Finally and inevitably, while operating on a young boy, unable to control his hands he severed an artery with fatal consequences.

Vilified by the local community, the former Doctor Hamilton found himself living in a disgusting one bedroom flat with his wife filing for divorce. It was at that point that he came to Liam

Donnelly's attention. They found that they could be mutually beneficial to each other. Donnelly had a use for a doctor that wouldn't ask any questions if needed either day, or more often at night, and Hamilton, unable to work, was grateful for the one hundred pounds per month retainer he received for services rendered.

Unwashed and unshaven, Hamilton now found himself on the Creggan estate at ten in the morning having received an urgent call to the pay phone on the landing of his apartment building. He opened the front door to the council house and went inside. Calling out to announce his arrival, he followed the responding voice down the hall and into a living room. Lying on the sofa, his shirt covered in blood, was Liam Donnelly. "About bloody time." he barked angrily pressing a small towel to his chest.

"What happened to you?"

"I've been shot, what does it bloody look like?" Hamilton removed the blood soaked towel and examined the wound.

"It doesn't look as if it has hit any of the major arteries. You were lucky. The bullet is still in there, I'll have to get it out. I don't have any anaesthetic so I'm afraid it's going to hurt."

"Just get on with it." Donnelly spat contemptuously. Two minutes of probing and pulling later, the bullet was out and Hamilton was suturing the wound. The pain must have been excruciating but Donnelly had barely made a sound save for the occasional grunt. This was a man clearly deserving of his reputation, Hamilton thought.

"You will need to rest for a few days; you've lost quite a lot of blood." Hamilton advised as he taped a dressing to the wound. Donnelly ignored the doctor's advice. He had more pressing matters to deal with.

Katie Preston pulled the Granada over to the kerb by the corrugated fence and stopped. She had made good time. It was eleven forty by the dashboard clock and she wasn't due to meet Prentiss for another twenty minutes. She knew that he would leave it until the last minute before he showed himself for fear of being arrested if spotted. She took the Walther PPK, the smaller of the two standard issue weapons used by Det operators, from beneath her seat, checked it and then put the weapon into her bag and got out of the car. She casually looked up and down the street. Except for the odd passing car, the street was quiet. Satisfied that she wasn't being watched, she squeezed through the gap in the fence and made her way across the former factory site.

She swore as her high heels sank into the muddy ground. There were times she missed wearing lightweights and combat boots. It took her a few minutes to find the sewer pipe that Prentiss had described to her over the phone. At last she saw it fifty yards to the left. Great, she thought, more rubble to climb over.

In the street outside, a white Austin Princess came to a stop fifty feet behind Preston's Granada on the other side of the road. Behind the wheel Jeremy Noble looked through the Granada's rear window with a small pair of binoculars. Confirming the car was empty, he then turned his attention to the gap in the corrugated fence. As he had followed Preston from Aldergrove to Londonderry he had gone over the night's events in his mind. He concluded that Prentiss, having been captured by Donnelly, must have escaped and was now meeting Preston to bring him in. As he had received no word from Donnelly regarding the money, he deduced that Prentiss must have hidden it before being picked up. He must now either be planning to retrieve it or had already done so. Either way Preston had unwittingly led him to his money. He thought for a moment then got out of the car and walked back to the telephone box he had passed at the end of the street. Once inside he dialled the memorised number and waited. An unfamiliar voice answered.

"Liam Donnelly." Noble's words were clipped. There was a pause.

"Donnelly."

"Did my man tell you where the money is before you let him escape?" Noble's voice was arrogant and condescending.

"Don't you start with me, soldier boy. I'm in no mood for it."

"No, I didn't think he would, self righteous little shit. Get yourself down to the site of the old cardboard factory. If he's not here already he will be very soon and he'll have the money with him."

"Don't kill him, he's mine. I'll be there in a few minutes."

Noble walked back down the street. Reaching the gap in the fence he pulled at it hard until two more of the rivets popped and he could fit through easily. Once inside he remained crouched and looked for movement. There was none. As he was about to stand a blonde head appeared a couple of hundred feet to his left. Preston clambered awkwardly over a pile of dirt and bricks hampered by the large attaché case she carried. Noble smiled as he went back through the fence and returned to his car.

Minutes later a dishevelled looking Lieutenant Preston appeared. She threw the case onto the back seat and got into the Granada. Taking her handkerchief she reached down under the steering wheel and began wiping the mud from her legs. Noble crossed the road to her car, approaching on her blind side so not to be detected. He pulled out a silenced PPK from beneath his jacket and got into the passenger seat beside her. Preston went for her bag but Noble snatched it away and threw it into the back next to the case.

"Aren't you a little old to be playing in the dirt, Lieutenant?" Noble mocked. Preston didn't reply. Her mind raced as she tried to think of a way of extricating herself from this situation. "Where is Prentiss?"

"No idea" she replied indignantly.

"He really is a remarkable young man, you know. I thought that he'd have been killed last night and I must admit it would have suited me if he had been. But he really is a capricious little bugger, isn't he? Far more resourceful than I ever gave him credit for. I must say, hiding the money did cause me quite a few problems but I'm glad to say it's all worked out in the end, thanks to you,

Lieutenant.

"You betrayed Michael to Donnelly when you found out he had taken the money. He trusted you."

"Well he's only got himself to blame. I told him quite specifically not to trust anyone. And I needed to get that money back."

"For your partner, Donnelly?" Preston said with disgust.

"Partner!" Noble laughed "Donnelly's not my partner. He's just a stupid Irish monkey that I used to get what I wanted. My dear girl, you don't really think I'd have dealings with scum like that unless I decided it was in my own interests to do so, do you? It was merely a necessary manipulation."

"And the oath you took when you became an officer to defend the crown against all enemies - that means nothing?"

"Look around you, Lieutenant. Do you really think we'll ever make any difference here? They couldn't hate us more if we walked down the street wrapped in the union flag singing God Save the Queen."

"So you've done all this just for the money."

"Lieutenant… Katie. A quarter of a million dollars in that case is mine. That gives me a new life somewhere where both the climate and the companionship are warm and exotic away from all this…filth. I realised a long time ago that there really was no future in being a man of honour and principle. So I decided to go into business for myself and nobody is going to stop me." Preston stared into Noble's eyes.

"What are you going to do now?"

"Well, clearly I can't let you live, now can I? You will only go tittle tattling to the Colonel and I really can't have that. Not after I've come so far. It's such a shame." Noble feigned a sad expression.

"You're just a petty thief."

"I can assure you young woman there is nothing petty about me."

Preston made a lunge for the gun but it coughed twice before she reached it. She slumped across Noble's lap. Hauling her body upright he placed her behind the wheel leaning against the door.

Retrieving the case from the back seat of the Granada, Noble casually walked back to the Princess. Placing the case on the passenger seat he opened it. He stared at the bundles of thousand dollar bills in front of him and touched them lightly with the palm of his hand. Then aware of his vulnerability began to remove half the bundles from the case and put them into a large navy blue holdall in the passenger floor well.

A brown Vauxhall Viva drove slowly past Preston's Granada and towards Noble's Princess. It was five minutes to twelve. Noble recognised the car and its driver and flashed his headlights. The Viva drew level with the Princess so that both the drivers were next to each other.

"Have you got the money?" Donnelly said, winding down his window. He didn't have the time or the inclination for pleasantries. Noble passed the attaché case through his window into Donnelly's hands.

"Where's your man?"

"He hasn't shown yet. His contact is in that light coloured Granada over there." Donnelly looked in his rear view mirror at the parked Ford. "Don't worry" continued Noble "I've taken care of her." He peered at Donnelly and with a supercilious tone said "You're looking rather peaky, are you sickening for something?" Donnelly sneered with contempt and stomped on the accelerator. The Viva set off with a squeal of tyres to the end of the road, turned around and made its way back parking a few feet opposite in front of the Granada. Donnelly switched off the engine and waited. Noble was intrigued to see how this played out so decided to remain, observing from his vantage point some distance away.

As Prentiss and Orla were approaching the area, inside the Granada Katie Preston murmured as she began to regain consciousness. Her face pallid from blood loss, she clutched her abdomen and tried in vain to reach her bag containing her radio. She fumbled for the door handle and pushed at the door. As it opened she fell out of the car onto the pavement crying out in pain. Noble gripped the steering wheel in a panic as he watched the woman who could identify him stagger to her feet. Across the road Donnelly was already out of his car with his pistol by his side and walking towards Preston. As he did so a blue mini turned into the end of the road. Prentiss recognised him instantly and shouted for Orla to stop the car. She pulled the car over and let the engine idle. Prentiss watched helplessly as Donnelly stood over Preston as she steadied herself on the Granada's front wing. Lifting his gun, he fired twice. Preston fell to the ground like a rag doll. Prentiss cried out and, reaching for his gun, started to open the door but Orla grabbed his arm and begged him not to.

"There's nothing you can do for her," she said. Tears of rage welled up in Prentiss' eyes as he pulled the door closed. They watched as Donnelly walked back to his car and got in. The shooting had caused the few passers by to run for cover. Donnelly knew it wouldn't be long before the whole area would be sealed off. He cursed, started the engine and drove towards the blue mini. Prentiss stared intently at Donnelly as he drove past.

"Follow him," he said quietly. As Orla turned the car to follow the Viva Prentiss took a last look at Katie's lifeless body lying crumpled on the pavement and vowed to avenge her.

In a white Austin Princess at the other end of the street Jeremy Noble smiled a sickly smile. Having watched the whole dramatic scene unobserved, he was now content that the young woman's death could not be connected to him. Moreover, as he watched the blue mini disappear from view, he knew that he only had to remain undiscovered for a few more hours. With Preston dealt with everything was once again going according to plan.

Chapter Fourteen

Liam Donnelly drove as quickly as the traffic allowed to the outskirts of the city. He pulled onto a shabby industrial estate and headed for 'Jim's Scrap Yard' at the far end. Splashing through the potholed entrance he pulled up next to a dented, filthy caravan. The site had thirty or so cars piled up one on top of the other in stacks of two or three. A large yellow crane with a four pronged grabber stood parked next to a long, red car crusher. A couple of men using cutting torches to break up a single decker bus, twisted and blackened by a petrol bomb attack a week earlier, created a cascade of yellow sparks.

Pulling the attaché case behind him, Donnelly stiffly climbed out of the car; his bullet wound clearly giving him pain. He called out loudly so as to be heard above the scrap yard noise and an old man appeared in the caravan doorway. He wore an aged, torn and dirty suit jacket over a green pullover, equally stained trousers and workman's steel toe-capped boots. The whole ensemble was topped off by a grey flat cap which reeked of rusting metal and tobacco. The man was in his late sixties; his face heavily lined and ingrained with black dirt. Recognising Donnelly he called his name, smiling to reveal the three remaining teeth in his head. Donnelly didn't return the smile; he merely pushed past and went inside the caravan.

"Have you got any whiskey?" Donnelly said sharply as he fell into the office chair.

"You're not looking so hot there, Liam. Are you alright?" the old man said, crossing to a filing cabinet and producing a half empty bottle of Jameson's. He poured a good slug into a chipped mugged and handed it over. Donnelly drank it down in one. That felt better; it took the edge off the pain.

"I'm grateful to you, Jim."

"What can I do for you?"

"I need you to get rid of the car outside, crush it so there's nothing left, understand?"

"Sure, Liam. No problem. Have you got the police after you?"

Donnelly ignored the question. "I need a van of some kind, doesn't need to be too big. Have you got anything like that?"

"I've a Morris Minor van round the back. It's a few years old now but the engine's sound enough."

"That'll do. I just need to lie low for a few hours then I'll be on my way."

"You can stay as long as you like, Liam, you know that. Is there anything else you need?"

Donnelly closed his eyes. "You can pour me another drink."

Parked on the main road at the entrance to the industrial estate, Prentiss and Orla sat in her blue mini having watched Donnelly drive into the scrap yard. They sat quietly, neither knowing what to say after witnessing Preston's murder. It was Orla who broke the silence. "So, who is this guy?"

Prentiss stared vacantly at the scrap yard. "A ghost" he

replied.

"What?"

"He's a terrorist called Liam Donnelly. He did all this." He waved his finger in front of his face. "I shot him when I escaped. I thought I'd killed him, obviously I didn't." There was another silence. Finally Orla's patience ran out.

"I think you'd better start telling me what's going on starting with who you are?" Prentiss looked at Orla. Every instinct was telling him not to draw this girl any further into this mess than he had to. However he did need her help and she had proved that he could trust her.

"My name is Michael Prentiss. I was recruited by an army intelligence unit to kill the man in the pub last night." He began slowly and gradually went on to explain the whole sequence of events from Noble's betrayal to his torture and subsequent escape. Orla sat wide eyed as she listened to Prentiss' incredible story.

"Why don't you contact your Colonel Maggot and expose this captain for what he is?"

Prentiss smiled painfully at Orla calling the Colonel 'Maggot'. The answer to her question was a complex one. For a start he had no idea where Mabbitt was and even if he did the question that worried him more that anything else was, was he complicit in it all? For the moment at least it would be better if he managed to stay under everybody's radar.

Colonel Mabbitt's Gazelle diverted before reaching

Aldergrove and touched down in Shackleton Barracks, Ballykelly, east of Londonderry. Having been informed of Lieutenant Preston's death in-flight back from London, he had given instructions that Captain Noble meet him at their northern base.

Still wearing his brown single breasted suit from his meeting earlier that day at MI5 headquarters in Gower Street, Mabbitt walked briskly into a ground floor office where Noble was waiting. Noble stood as the Colonel entered the room. "What the hell is going on?" Mabbitt demanded, his voice uncharacteristically raised and emotional.

"You mean Lieutenant Preston, Sir?"

"Don't be obtuse, Jeremy. Yes dammit I mean Lieutenant Preston. I leave her here twelve hours ago in comms and return to find her shot dead on a Londonderry street." Mabbitt fumed.

"The lieutenant received a personal telephone call earlier this morning while she was in the communications room from someone purporting to be her brother."

"She didn't have a brother." Mabbitt replied quickly.

"Quite."

"Do we know who it was, this caller?"

"No." Noble's voice was cold and completely without emotion. "Naturally I was suspicious, particularly when I asked her to whom she was speaking and she said she was ringing here to get an update regarding Prentiss." Noble paused but Mabbitt said nothing so he continued. "She said she was tired and asked permission to return to her quarters to get some sleep. Instead she

Assassin's Run

booked out a car and I followed her to Londonderry. It was there that she met Liam Donnelly to receive what looked like some kind of pay-off."

"Donnelly? And you saw this pay-off?" Mabbitt asked in astonishment.

"Yes, Sir. Unfortunately for Preston, Donnelly had other ideas and killed her."

"Where is he now?"

"We don't know, surveillance on The Anchor reports that he didn't return there."

"And Prentiss? Any word from him?"

"No, nothing. I'm afraid it's not looking too good for him. We have to consider the possibility that he has been killed." Noble replied earnestly.

"What a mess." Mabbitt rubbed his cheeks with his palms.

"Why did they want you in Gower Street?" Noble asked innocently.

"Thank you, Jeremy that will be all." Mabbitt had no intention of discussing the matter. Noble nodded and left, satisfied with his performance but perturbed by his CO's unwillingness to confide in him. Mabbitt sat in his chair dolefully. He found it hard to accept that Katie Preston, one of his best operators, had been a traitor. His mind then turned to Prentiss. Surely he would have found some way of contacting the unit. Having the intelligence and the guile to successfully complete such a difficult mission only to disappear completely made no sense at all. Mabbitt frowned and reached for the telephone. Having asked the communications operator to connect him with Templar Barracks, he waited impatiently, tapping his finger on the desk until a voice answered.

"Sergeant Jordan, please." Another pause as the call was routed through to Repton Manor. Jordan answered.

"Richard." Jordan recognised the voice to be that of his commanding officer and replied with a clipped "Sir."

"We've got some problems here. I think you had better come over."

"Yes, Sir. What sort of problems?"

"Katie's dead and Michael is missing."

"Understood. I'll chopper out within the hour and be with you by five."

"No, I want you to fly into Belfast Palace Barracks. Contact me directly at Aldergrove when you get there, and Richard; let's keep your visit confidential, just between us."

Outside the industrial estate Prentiss and Orla were still maintaining their vigil on the scrap yard. Orla, a naturally bright and vivacious girl, felt uncomfortable with the awkward silences that punctuated their conversations. Prentiss fixed his eyes on the scrap yard entrance scrutinising every movement. Tentatively Orla broached the subject of Katie Preston. "The girl that was killed, were you very close?"

"I only met her a week ago but yes, she was…a friend. I never considered until now how much we take life for granted.

You get up in the morning assuming that you'll get through the day and then go to bed that night ready to do it all over again the following day. Although her job was dangerous I don't suppose Katie thought for one minute that she wouldn't be going to bed tonight. I can't help thinking that if I'd have made sure Donnelly was dead in that kitchen she would still be alive."

"It's not your fault; it's the way it is here."

"But why is it, I don't understand?"

"Eleven years ago the IRA were split into two; the Dublin based 'officials', who's aim was a united socialist Ireland through peaceful means, and the Provisionals, based in Belfast who also wanted a unified Ireland but used violence as the catalyst. Initially the Provos got little support for their random bombings and sniper attacks then in January 1972 it all changed. I was only twelve but I remember it like it was yesterday. The British army opened fire on a catholic rally here in Londonderry. Fourteen unarmed people were killed. It was just what the Provos had been waiting for. From then on the Provos' numbers grew and grew and the 'officials' just disappeared into obscurity. It was later that year that they went on a bombing spree in Belfast detonating twenty-two bombs in just over an hour. Nine dead and one hundred and thirty injured. So you see, Michael, none of us here take it for granted that we will get through the day. We just thank god when we do."

Prentiss didn't have the words to adequately express how he felt. He couldn't begin to comprehend how anyone could live a normal life here and could only look on in admiration at Orla and all those like her who did. It only affirmed his deSire to stop Liam Donnelly doing whatever it was he was about to do.

Thirty minutes later, at two-fifteen, Colonel Mabbitt flew out of Ballykelly and returned to Aldergrove. Captain Noble remained with orders to find Prentiss no matter what. He sat in a small office, the navy blue holdall secreted under the desk by his leg. He closed his eyes deep in thought. Prentiss running around unchecked could prove to be a problem. He could no longer rely on Donnelly getting rid of him but Prentiss was a variable that required attention. His mind was taken back to the street in which Preston was shot and the blue mini with Prentiss in the passenger seat. "The resourceful little sod has enlisted some civilian help," considered Noble. He opened his eyes. Picking up the phone he asked for an outside line and began dialling. During his time in the province Noble had made a great many useful contacts in most of the RUC departments and it was to one of these he was about to use.

Mary Laughlin was a plain looking woman on the wrong side of forty. She was a large woman, not fat but certainly what might be called robust. Never having so much as a serious boyfriend let alone having got married, she, as the eternal optimist, constantly lived in hope of romance. She was therefore excited and flattered when a charming and rather dashing British army captain started buying her coffee on a regular basis at a local Belfast café. Although their relationship had never progressed beyond small talk within the confines of the café, Mary was certain that it was only going to be a matter of time before this man would pluck up the courage to reveal his true feelings for her. All because of a chance meeting a year ago, she would often muse, when he visited the police headquarters where she worked and took an interest in her work with the police national computer.

At her desk at police headquarters, Mary Laughlin stopped typing and answered her telephone. Her face glowed at hearing the caller's voice and she smoothed her thick black hair from her face with her palm. "Jeremy, how lovely to hear from you," she cooed. She listened attentively as Noble asked her for 'a huge favour'.

"I shouldn't really, Jeremy. It's against the rules." Her breathing quickened at the promise of dinner on Saturday night if she would just do this one little thing for him.

"Oh alright give me the registration number." As she listened Mary typed in the registration number of the blue mini. Within seconds Orla Duncan's details popped up on her screen. Mary read out the name and address in a hushed voice so as not to be overheard.

Having promised to ring Mary at the end of the week to arrange their dinner date, Noble replaced the receiver, tore the page from the notepad on his desk and smiled. He found exploiting people's weaknesses very satisfying, he thought to himself, just one of the many benefits of having no conscience.

The small clock on the dashboard of Orla's mini showed

three o'clock. "How much longer are we going to sit here?" she said, beginning to doubt if Donnelly was ever going to come out of the scrap yard. Prentiss glanced down at the clock.

"I don't suppose it will be too much longer."

"But it's been over two hours, what if he doesn't come out?"

"He'll come out." Prentiss said assuredly.

"How do you know?"

"When I was being 'questioned' I heard them talking as I was coming round from being knocked unconscious. Something about the delivery is set for ten o'clock tonight. All Donnelly was interested in was where I'd hidden the money, not who I was or who I was working for. Katie was going to pick it up before she brought me in so he must now have it. Therefore we can safely assume that he will be keeping his appointment at ten o'clock tonight."

"What sort of delivery is it?"

"I don't know. It's very important to Donnelly, I know that much."

"So what are you going to do?"

"Whatever it takes to stop him getting it."

Chapter Fifteen

Captain Noble made his way across the base at Ballykelly from his office to the armoury, acknowledging salutes from the occasional serviceman he passed on the way. He strutted into the armoury and stood by the door. Behind a long counter a sergeant busied himself with the sports pages of a newspaper while noisily slurping the last dregs of his tea mug. The sergeant jumped to attention as Noble slammed the door behind him announcing his arrival.

"I'm not disturbing you, am I, sergeant?" Noble sneered.

"Yes, Sir. I mean no, Sir. What can I do for you, Sir." Most of the servicemen that knew Captain Noble were fully aware of the consequences of incurring the man's wrath.

"Where is the Sarn't Major?"

"He's stepped out for a moment, Sir. Should be back in five minutes."

"I want to see him now, go and get him."

"I'm sorry, Sir; I'm not supposed to leave the armoury unattended."

"It won't be unattended will it? I am here! Now go and get him!" Noble bellowed.

"Yes, Sir, straight away, Sir." The sergeant doubled round the counter and out of the armoury door. Once he was alone, Noble quickly walked behind the counter and down the long rows of rifle racks. At the far end, separate to the main armoury, was an area where seized terrorist weapons were stored before being destroyed.

Noble looked carefully at the array of Armalites, handguns and ammunition until he found what he had come for. On a metal table there were half a dozen small packages wrapped in brown grease proof paper. He picked one up and looked at the label 'Explosive plastic SEMTEX H'. This three pound block alone could easily destroy a two storey building. Terrorists around the world now preferred the Czech-made plastic explosive rather than dynamite as it was odourless, easily concealed and far more destructive. He slipped it into his jacket pocket together with a couple of small silver rods each fitted with a long red wire. Casually Noble left the armoury building and walked back to the administration block. Minutes later, having collected his holdall from the office, he was in his car and driving the fifteen miles to Londonderry.

It was just before four o'clock when Noble parked his white Princess opposite Orla Duncan's flat. On entering the building it didn't take him long to locate her front door on the first floor. The landing was clear and he wasted no time picking the lock and letting himself inside. During his career Noble had done this many times when either planting listening devices or searching for information. He walked down the hall, looking in each room as he passed, until he got to the kitchen.

Standing in the centre of the kitchen, Noble slowly looked about him until he saw a large metal biscuit tin on top of the wall cupboard. Reaching up he lifted it down and opened it. Inside he found the tin to be half full of assorted biscuits and cookies. Taking out a chocolate one and holding it in his mouth he tipped the rest into the kitchen bin. Taking out the plastic explosive and detonators from his pocket he placed them into the empty tin and returned it to the top of the cupboard.

Noble finished eating his biscuit as he made his way back down the hallway towards the front door. As he did so he heard the unmistakable sound of a key in the lock. As the front door opened he slipped into a bedroom closing the door until it was open an inch. "Orla, are you home?" Noble watched as a young brunette girl wearing a nurse's uniform beneath her unbuttoned coat walked past the bedroom and into the kitchen. Noble thought for a moment then looked around the bedroom. A red silk scarf hung on the end of the bed. He picked it up and went out into the hallway. Winding the ends of the scarf tightly around each hand as he entered the kitchen, Noble moved silently towards the girl as she sat at the table with her back to him. Like a cobra he struck. Slipping it around her throat, he tightened the scarf, squeezing the life from the girl. With her petite frame and seated position she couldn't resist Noble's strength, frantically trying in vain to grab at his forearms behind her. Within seconds she made a last choking sound. Noble released his grip, her head falling back on the chair. He tossed the scarf onto the table and, as calmly as he had entered, he left the flat pleased with the unexpected additional element to his plan.

Returning to his car he drove for a few minutes before pulling over next to a call box. He dialled 999 and in a thick Belfast accent asked for the police. Once connected he explained that he had seen the gunman who shot that American in the pub last night they were looking for. Giving the registration number he described the blue mini that had almost run him over on the outskirts of Londonderry. Once he was asked who and where he was Noble hung up. This wouldn't be considered as unusual since almost all the tip offs the police received were anonymous for fear of reprisal. Lifting the receiver again Noble dialled the communications room at Aldergrove smiling as he did so. Once connected he blurted out in a panic stricken voice "This is Noble, they're after me, they're after..." and hung up, his smile returning. As he got back into the car Noble was satisfied that everything was in place. It was now only a matter of time before Prentiss was out of the way. There was only one more piece of the jigsaw to put into place.

Noble's 999 telephone call had started the sequence of events he both anticipated and required. The RUC, having got Orla's personal details and address from a search of the registration number anonymously supplied by Noble, sent two police Land Rovers to her flat. Having smashed their way in, they discovered the body of her flatmate in the kitchen. The subsequent search tore apart the flat. It wasn't long before the Semtex and detonators concealed in the biscuit tin were discovered together with Prentiss' blood stained clothes in the bedroom. That was enough for an all cars alert to apprehend the occupants of the blue mini under the special powers terrorism act. With the probability that they were armed terrorists and would resist arrest, extreme caution was to be used.

Colonel Mabbitt's private secure line was ringing as he returned to his office in Aldergrove from the communications centre. Richard Jordan had just flown in from Ashford and was calling from Palace Barracks in Belfast.

"Richard, I'm glad you're here. I could use your expertise." Mabbitt said, his voice sounding tired and drained.

"What happened to Lieutenant Preston?"

"That's rather unclear at present. On the face of it she was killed by Donnelly rather than receiving payment for services rendered."

"I can't believe that, Sir. Katie was no traitor."

"I agree with you, Richard. There's more going on here than just a terrorist being bankrolled."

"What do you need me to do?"

"I'd like you to have a little chat with a Peter Collins, an MI5 desk officer in Belfast. Find out who the source of his information was regarding Donald Boyle funding Donnelly. I'm intrigued to know as I thought that we had exclusivity on that piece of intelligence."

"Is this an official chat?"

"No, I think he'll be more forthcoming if you speak to him on a strictly informal basis. I'm certain with your people skills he'll tell you what we need to know."

"I'll take care of it."

"Oh, Richard, one more thing. I've just learned that the police have a lead on Michael. He appears to have enlisted some help from a young woman, Orla Duncan; they are both being sought on terrorism charges. For the moment at least we know that he's still alive. I will keep you apprised of any developments." Jordan thanked him and assured the Colonel that he'd be in touch.

Peter Collins steered his yellow Triumph TR7 aggressively through the hectic Belfast rush hour traffic. He was on his way home for a quick shower, change of clothes and then a hot date with the lovely Megan, a giggly blonde barmaid he met at his local pub. Her lack of intelligence, or grasp of reality if it came to that, was more than compensated by her ample bosom and willing disposition.

Collins had been recruited by MI5 when he was studying anthropology at the University of Ulster. Now, at twenty-five, he was an ambitious desk officer running three informants in the province. An incorrigible womaniser, his activities had attracted the attention of the security section who were concerned that he may become the target of a honey trap. A technique used to great effect during the cold war was still widely used, exploiting sexual weakness to blackmail the subject for sensitive information. Following a stern warning from his superior, Collins was strongly advised to curb his indiscriminate intimate liaisons with complete strangers if he wanted to keep his positive vetting certificate and remain in the service.

The TR7 screeched to halt at the side of the road outside Collins' house. Turning off the engine he caught sight of himself in the rear view mirror and flicked his long dark fringe back into place with his fingertips. In doing so he didn't notice Richard Jordan approaching on the footpath. Jordan deftly opened the passenger door and got in beside a startled Collins. "Who the bloody hell are you? Get out of my car."

"Calm yourself, Peter; I just want to ask you a few questions." Collins reached for his door handle but Jordan gripped his arm, twisting it at the wrist. Collins cried out in pain as Jordan maintained pressure on his arm.

"Who are you, what do you want?" Jordan relaxed his grip.

"That's better. Now, I want you to tell me the name of your informant who gave you the Donald Boyle information."

"I don't know what you're talking about." Collins replied. Jordan re-tightened his grip on the man's arm causing him to cry out again.

"Trust me, sonny I've been doing this a long time and I am very good at it. You really don't want this to move on to the next stage. Now who was the informant?"

"I can't; I'm under orders." Jordan twisted again. "Please you're hurting my arm!"

"I'll break it if you don't tell me. The name?" Collins writhed around in his seat.

"Jeremy Noble, it was Jeremy Noble." Jordan released Collins' arm. "He's an officer in army intelligence. It was him who told me that Boyle was planning to support Donnelly." Collins was no hero. He was prepared to spill the lot.

"How do you know Jeremy Noble?"

"I met him when he was on secondment to 'five', we keep in touch."

"Why would he tell you about Boyle and Donnelly?"

"I suppose he felt that it would help inter-agency relations." Jordan knew that Noble couldn't care less about inter-agency relations.

"You said that you were under orders, who's? Noble?"

"No, Dominic Fellows, Head of Northern Ireland Section." Collins replied rubbing his painful arm.

"Did you file a report?"

"No, Noble told me to keep it completely unofficial."

"So, you told your boss who sent it up the line to Fellows giving you the credit for getting the information from one of your informants."

"No, I by-passed the local office and took it straight to Fellows."

"Why?"

"Jeremy said that was the best way to play it." Jordan could see what was emerging and wanted clarification.

"You mean Noble told you to take the information directly to Fellows, no-one else?"

Collins nodded. "Do Fellows and Noble know each other?" Collins shrugged

"I dunno, maybe."

"Did Noble tell you that an operation was going to be mounted to kill Boyle?"

"Yes."

"When?"

"About a week before."

"And you passed that on to Fellows too?" Collins nodded.

"I was surprised that Fellows let it go ahead. I thought he'd be throwing his weight around when he found out about an operation, an illegal operation at that, on his patch but he told me to keep it to myself. It's not like him at all." Jordan thought for a moment then turned to Collins menacingly.

"This conversation never took place, understand?" Collins nodded.

"You're one of those funny ones aren't you, like Noble?"

"Trust me, there's nothing funny about me." Jordan got out of the yellow sports car.

"No, I can believe that." Collins said to himself as he watched him walk away.

In Jim's scrap yard Liam Donnelly washed down some painkillers with the last of the Jameson's. He felt better after resting up for a few hours in the caravan 'office'. His brown Viva had been crushed as he had ordered. All that remained was a brown metal cube lost in a large pile of unidentifiable scrap metal.

"It's time I was going. You're a good man, Jim, so you are."

Donnelly shook the old man's shoulder.

"Where will you go now?"

"It's better that you don't know." He picked up the attaché case. Jim handed him the keys to the van.

"Whatever it is you're doing, I wish you well." The scrap dealer had long since been a supporter of the IRA and a friend to Liam Donnelly. Thirteen years earlier he had been active in the Northern Ireland Civil Rights Association demanding an end to the discrimination against the catholic population. He himself had been viciously attacked by the RUC, an almost completely protestant police force, while on a civil march. These repeated attacks on marches culminated in the Battle of the Bogside, a three day riot between the RUC and the catholic residents in Londonderry.

Outside the industrial estate Prentiss and Orla took it in turns to get out of the cramped confines of the car and stretch their legs. While one walked up and down the road, the other kept watch on the entrance to the scrap yard. Prentiss looked at the time, six-fifteen. After more than five hours Prentiss was beginning to wonder whether Donnelly had managed to get out of the scrap yard by an alternative route. Orla sat hunched against the door, her head resting on the window fast asleep. There had been a brief flurry of activity at six o'clock as workers from the other unit on the estate had finished for the day. Prentiss had scrutinised the occupants of every vehicle as it pulled out onto the road but Donnelly wasn't in any of them. Since then there had been almost nothing.

Prentiss pulled down the sun visor revealing a small mirror.

The cut under his eye was stinging as the blue-green bruising spread around the swelling. As he examined the wound he was aware of movement from the estate. He flicked up the visor to see a black Morris Minor van slowly emerging from the scrap yard. As he watched the van he gently shook Orla's arm and told her to wake up. She did so with a start.

"What is it?" she asked looking at Prentiss who was staring intently at something, narrowing his eyes trying to focus. As the black van drew closer Prentiss felt his heart begin to beat faster with a combination of excitement and relief.

"That's him." he whispered. Orla went to start the engine. "No wait, starting the engine will draw his attention over here." The van stopped briefly at the entrance to the estate. Donnelly looked around briefly then pulled out and drove away from them. "Right, let's go but keep well back."

"I know, I watch television too." She pulled the mini out into the road and began to follow Donnelly out of the city.

Chapter Sixteen

Once back at Palace Barracks, Richard Jordan found a quiet office with a secure telephone line and rang Colonel Mabbitt at Aldergrove.

"Ah Richard, have you spoken to Collins?" Mabbitt said brightly as he heard Jordan's voice.

"Yes, Sir. As you suspected, there's more going on here than meets the eye."

"Explain."

"Collins didn't get his information from an informant but from Captain Noble."

"Did he now?"

"It gets better. Noble also told him about Operation Ares over a week ago - that's before Prentiss had even been recruited. Noble told him to take the information directly to the Head of the Northern Ireland Section, Dominic Fellows, and not to mention it to anyone else." Mabbitt didn't reply. He sat silently considering this latest information and reflecting on that morning's meeting with Fellows.

"What do you think Captain Noble's playing at, Sir?"

"That remains to be seen, Richard. Captain Noble appears to have gone missing. He left Ballykelly a little after three. We received some garbled message from him a little later that someone was after him but nothing since. He's not responding to his radio and the tracker on his car has been disabled."

"Has he been snatched?"

"Time will tell on that one, Richard but I'm not convinced his call was all that it appeared."

"Do you think he killed Katie?"

"No, eyewitness reports have identified Liam Donnelly as the shooter - that much is certain. What is far less certain is Captain Noble's involvement."

"Do you need me to come there?" Jordan asked.

"No, stay in Belfast for the moment but be ready to move quickly. The good captain clearly has a private agenda. What concerns me is what his next move will be."

Jeremy Noble had driven out of the city and was gently stirring a cup of rather weak coffee at a food stained table in a roadside café south of Londonderry. The air was thick with the smell of fried food and cigarette smoke. He sat by the window facing the door so he could see anyone approaching. As the fluorescent light above him highlighted the grease floating on the top of the swirling liquid, Noble decided against drinking the coffee and, pushing it away, looked at his watch. Five to seven, time to make a phone call. Asking the passing waitress if there was a public phone, he was directed through a swing door into a corridor where one hung on the wall.

In Dominic Fellows office in MI5's Gower Street headquarters, the phone on his red leather topped desk rang. Answering with his usual superior tone, Fellows leant back in his chair as the caller spoke. "Jeremy, this is unexpected. What can I do for you?"

"It's more what I can do for you, Dominic. How did your little chat with my beloved leader go this morning?"

"I don't know how you can bear to work for that self-righteous little tic, Jeremy, but don't worry; I'll bring him down a peg or two when I launch an official inquiry into yesterday's débâcle."

"I might be able to help you there. Is this a secure line?" Fellows turned to the telephone on his desk and pressed a button that illuminated red.

"It is now. What are you up to, Jeremy?" Fellows asked suspiciously.

"I've been thinking for a while that it's time for a change. I was considering coming back to 'five' but it would need to be a favourable position."

"Favourable?"

"Yes someone with influence in the service would need to put a word in, as it were."

"And you think I have that much influence?"

"You will have, Dominic. Your rise through the service is about to become meteoric and as a little bonus you'll finish Charles Mabbitt and his unruly bunch of cowboys permanently." As the master of manipulation, Noble had succeeded in whetting Fellows' thirst for ambition. "You see, Dominic, you are about to save the life of the Prime Minister." Fellows didn't reply. Noble knew from his silence that he had his fish hooked.

Noble spent the next ten minutes reeling in Dominic Fellows. He explained that he had intelligence that Liam Donnelly was planning an assassination attempt on the Prime Minister during her secret visit to Northern Ireland the following day. Scheduled for almost a month, Margaret Thatcher had expressed a wish to visit the troops in the province. A wish reinforced by the events of the Iranian Embassy siege earlier that month. The hit was to be made at RAF Aldergrove, ironically right under Colonel Mabbitt's nose, using a long range sniper. Fellows sat in silence as Noble gently advised him to secretly change the PM's venue to probably the safest place in the province, Thiepval Barracks, Lisburn, the British Army Headquarters in Northern Ireland. As a further precaution she should travel by Wessex helicopter rather than air force jet. The jet should still fly into Aldergrove as planned, now however as a diversion so as not to alert the sniper that there had been a change.

Having agreed to follow Noble's plan, Fellows sat in his office with a smug expression on his face. He could see it now, an assassination attempt foiled, the PM's life saved and a deadly terrorist caught. This would surely guarantee promotion not to mention considerable kudos in the service and the personal gratitude of the Prime Minister. Then, of course, there was the delicious gift of the downfall of Charles Mabbitt. He would have achieved all this without Mabbitt even knowing it was taking place. This would certainly diminish if not destroy the Colonel's standing in the intelligence community, proving him to be impotent when it came to gathering vital intelligence. It would be Dominic Fellows that would emerge triumphant and to him that important eyes would turn regarding all intelligence matters in Northern Ireland.

Fellows picked up the phone. He didn't think it a good idea to have Jeremy Noble back in the service. That may prove to be a rather difficult relationship as he had no intention of giving him any credit for this piece of intelligence. It was too bad for poor Jeremy, Fellows considered as he dialled, because he had proved to be very useful in the past but he had simply outlived his usefulness and it was time for him to be cut loose. Clearly this information needed to come from MI5. Fellows finished dialling and waited. Finally Fellows said "Is that Peter Collins?"

Michael Prentiss and Orla Duncan had been following Liam Donnelly for almost an hour. Orla had become quite skilled in keeping at least one car between them and Donnelly's van. They had travelled south, alternating between quiet country roads and the busy main arterial routes. Wherever he was going Donnelly was clearly avoiding the army checkpoints. Up ahead was a large service station. The indicator on Donnelly's van came on. Orla slowed. "What do we do?" she asked as the Morris Minor van turned off the road onto the covered forecourt, coming to a stop at a petrol pump.

"Follow him in," Prentiss said scouring the forecourt for somewhere to go. "There." he pointed to the parking area of a small café that adjoined the petrol station some distance from where Donnelly had stopped. Orla nosed the mini into a space between two cars and turned off the engine. Prentiss watched out of the back window as Donnelly filled the van with fuel. As he watched, an RUC Land Rover turned onto the forecourt and slowly drove past the pumps towards where they were parked. Donnelly eyed the Land Rover casually but the two officers inside didn't even look in his direction. They were concentrating on the parking area near the café. Prentiss turned away as the officer in the passenger seat made eye contact with Orla.

"They're looking at us," she whispered as the police vehicle continued past and out of the service station. "I thought they were going to stop for a minute there; he was looking right at me." Orla said, smiling with relief. Prentiss looked concerned.

"I don't like it; we need to leave the car."

"But they've gone."

"Come on!" Prentiss got out of the car, keeping low so Donnelly didn't see him. Moving round the front of the mini, he grabbed Orla's hand as she stood by the door and they ran towards the café. Prentiss led them into a narrow space behind the café between the back wall of the building and an overgrown conifer hedge. Once they were concealed he turned to see the police Land Rover return, hurtling across the forecourt and coming to a screeching halt immediately behind Orla's mini. With their weapons drawn the two officers leapt from their vehicle and stood either side of the little car.

Donnelly finished at the pump and walked with his head bowed the short distance to the garage to pay. As he did so he watched one of the police officers search the car while the other spoke into his radio. Such occurrences weren't unusual and Donnelly knew that so long as he didn't attract attention to himself they wouldn't give him a second look.

From their hiding place Prentiss and Orla watched the police scan the open fields behind the service station. Unable to spot their terrorist suspects the two officers charged into the café pushing aside a rather scruffy sales rep returning to his car as they did so. With his protestations ignored the pot-bellied Irishman lumbered back to his Volvo estate adjusting his crumpled brown suit jacket. As he got into his car Donnelly appeared from the garage and walked back to the van.

"He's leaving, Michael. What do we do?" whispered Orla. Prentiss watched the sales rep looking at a map in his car as Donnelly drove across the forecourt.

"Come on." Prentiss took Orla's hand and they ran to the far end of the café wall. This brought them outside the service station boundary. Prentiss could see Donnelly's van pull out onto the road to his right. Running up the side of the café and adjoining garage they were now close to the service station exit. Prentiss turned to Orla.

"There will be a fat bloke in a Volvo estate come out of here in a minute. I want you to use your charm and flag him down." Prentiss waited by the building as Orla walked up to the exit. Sure enough, the sales rep appeared at the exit a few seconds later. Orla waved to him, giving her 'I'm so helpless' smile. Leaning over, he wound down the window and asked if he could help. While she asked for a lift Prentiss, his approach obscured by Orla, got into the back seat and pressed his gun into the folds of the rep's neck. Orla got into the passenger seat. "Drive." Prentiss hissed pushing the Beretta harder into the man's flesh. The terrified rep managed to mumble "okay" and pulled out of the service station.

"Put your foot down; we're in a hurry." Prentiss said, his mouth close to the driver's ear. There wasn't too much traffic on the road and Prentiss 'encouraged' the sales rep to overtake anything in front of them.

After five minutes Orla cried "There!" and pointed to the familiar rear double doors of the black Morris Minor in the distance.

"See that van?" Prentiss said. The driver nodded. "I want you to follow it but stay back; I don't want him to know we're here. Got it?" He nodded again.

As they settled down to following Donnelly again, the sales rep glanced at Prentiss in the rear view mirror and then across at Orla. She noticed him looking at her.

"What?" she said. The rep gathered some courage.

"You're the two from the news, aren't you? The ones the police are looking for. You killed that nurse in Derry." Orla turned to him.

"What nurse?"

"The nurse you strangled in her own kitchen, Suzanne something." Orla gasped and put her hands to her mouth

"Suzy."

"Every copper in Northern Ireland is looking for you. They found all of your bomb making stuff as well."

"Bomb making? Michael, what's he talking about?"

"I don't know but I can guess. You've been set up, we both have."

"Who would kill Suzy, how do they even know I'm helping you?" her voice was growing increasingly frantic.

"We must have been seen together. Somebody is going to a lot of trouble to stop me. Did you see those coppers back there? They were ready to shoot first and worry about the consequences later."

"Who are you? They said on the news that you killed those two Americans in Londonderry. You're supposed to be French or something. You don't sound very French to me." The rep's eyes flicked up to the mirror to see Prentiss staring at the van ahead as he replied.

"Me? I'm nobody, nobody at all."

"Look all I want to do is get home. I don't want to get mixed up with whatever it is you two are into." The rep was beginning to wish he had kept his mouth shut.

"What's your name?" Prentiss asked.

"Gordon" he replied.

"Listen, Gordon, just do what I say and you'll soon be home.

We don't want to hurt you. Believe me, all any of us want to do is just to go home."

"That's easy for you to say. You haven't got a gun stuck in your ear."

The three continued in silence for another twenty minutes then, up ahead, Donnelly's van turned off the main road onto a smaller country lane. It was more difficult for the Volvo to remain undetected as these lanes had very little traffic. Fortunately it was almost sunset; another thirty minutes and it would be dark. Gordon's fear was getting the better of him and his constant nervous chatter was becoming irritating. Finally Prentiss had had enough. "Pull over here."

"Why?"

"Just do it, now!" Gordon pulled the car over onto the grass verge.

"Don't you want to keep following the van?"

"Out!" Prentiss ordered getting out of the car and opening the driver's door. Gordon raised his hands as he saw the gun in Prentiss' hand pointed at him.

"Are you going to shoot me?" Prentiss grabbed the man's jacket lapel and hauled him out of the car onto the road.

"Take off your shoes."

"My shoes?"

"I'm having a really bad day and I don't have time to waste so take them off!" Hurriedly Gordon took off the brown loafers. Prentiss picked them up and threw them into the back of the car.

"Orla, get behind the wheel. Now listen, Gordon. You should be able to get a lift where we turned off," Prentiss said as he walked round to the passenger door.

"But that's miles. It'll take me hours!" exclaimed Gordon as he stood uncomfortably on the rough ground. Prentiss smiled.

"That's the idea. Anyway, the exercise will do you good." He got into the car and Orla hit the accelerator, spinning the wheels and causing stones and dust to fly into the air as they sped off down the lane.

"I've only had that car a fortnight!" Gordon yelled defiantly after them but they were already out of sight.

Chapter Seventeen

A little before nine-thirty Liam Donnelly drove onto the disused former RAF airfield at Cluntoe. Located a mile or so from the banks of Lough Neagh, the largest lake in the British Isles and near the village of Ardboe, it had been left abandoned for years. Cluntoe was used firstly by the USAF during World War Two to train B-24 Liberator heavy bomber crews, then briefly by the RAF as the Number Two Flying Training School before being closed in 1955.

A couple of minutes later Orla parked the Volvo a little way down a wooded track opposite the airfield entrance. It had been dark for half an hour and so they wouldn't be seen. Orla had followed Donnelly without using the headlights. Catching only the occasional glimpse of the van's two little red tail lights to guide her, Orla's eyes were now sore with concentration. Prentiss had been quiet. The gnawing pain from the wound in his mouth was increasing. He bit down hard on the broken tooth to try and ease the pain but only succeeded in causing the gum to start bleeding again. He swore as he opened the door and spat out the blood. Orla reached for her bag and took out a bottle of pills. With the interior light illuminated she could see Prentiss clearly and winced. With blood coming from his mouth and the various cuts and bruises on his face swelling and discoloured, he looked a mess. She opened the bottle and handed it to him. "Here take these, it'll ease the pain."

"Thanks." Prentiss poured out half a dozen into the palm of

his hand and tossed them onto the back of his throat. He washed them down with what was left of a bottle of cola that lay on the back seat amongst assorted packs of sandwiches, crisps and biscuits. One thing you could say for Gordon, Prentiss thought, he did keep a well stocked car. Orla, realising she hadn't eaten anything since breakfast, devoured a pack of ham sandwiches with vigour.

Prentiss wiped the blood from his mouth with the back of his hand and took out the gun he had taken from Finton. It was a Browning Hi-power 9mm, the same type as he had used the first day at Ashford on the CQB course. He pressed the small button behind the trigger ejecting the magazine; it was almost full. He pushed it back in, flicked on the safety catch with his thumb and put the big automatic in his pocket. Prentiss then took out his Beretta and examined its magazine. There were two rounds, with another in the chamber making three. "Good," he thought. Slamming the magazine back in with the heel of his hand, he held it out to Orla. "I want you to take this." Orla, having watched Prentiss check the weapons, stopped chewing her sandwich and stared at the little gun.

"I, I can't. I mean I've never even fired a gun."

"It's easy, you just point and shoot."

"No, I despise guns. I don't want it," she said, shaking her head.

"Listen, I need to go in there and see what Donnelly is up to but it's safer if you stay here. I want you to have it… just in case."

They looked at each other in silence for a moment. Prentiss then got out of the car leaving the gun on the passenger seat behind him, shut the door and ran off towards the airfield entrance. Orla looked at the Beretta and turned away from it then thought for a few seconds. She looked down at the polished black gun again then tentatively picked it up and felt the weight of it in her hand. She rested it in her lap and sat nervously in the car, staring into the dark.

The headlights of the Morris Minor van momentarily lit up the derelict former control tower building as it swung round and faced the runway. Donnelly lit a cigarette and then held his watch up to the lighter flame, nine thirty-five. Leaving the headlights on, he got out of the van and looked up at the sky. It was a dark night. The gentlest of breezes barely moved the dense cloud obscuring any chance of a glimpse of moonlight to illuminate the airfield. Donnelly stood leaning with his back against the van and looked up at the building in front of him. The windows were covered with metal shutters, the brick walls flaking and weather beaten with age and the maroon painted door was secured with a large brass padlock.

Prentiss could see the van's lights in the distance. Staying low, he sprinted between the buildings, using them for cover. He could just make out Donnelly's silhouette behind the van and the occasional orange glow as he drew on his cigarette. Prentiss was about a hundred feet from him now, crouching behind a small store building. He was deciding whether he could chance getting any closer when he saw another pair of headlights approaching from the main road. As the vehicle approached Prentiss was aware that he was going to be visible to the driver in just a few seconds and so scurried around the building until it passed.

The white wedge-shaped saloon stopped next to the van and a tall thin figure got out. Prentiss, still in his crouched position, peered round the corner of the building. As the driver walked round the front of his car his face was lit for a second in the lights.

"Noble, you treacherous..." Prentiss muttered to himself recognising the man who had been so friendly to him the week before at Ashford and ironically had told him to 'trust no-one.' Little could he have imagined that this was the person he shouldn't have trusted. Prentiss cast his mind back to the previous Thursday and his brief chat with Katie in the firing range at Repton Manor. She knew there was something untrustworthy about him. He couldn't get her lovely blue eyes out of his head. The memory of seeing her shot dead in the street haunted him. Donnelly may have been the one that pulled the trigger but Noble was complicit and for that he would have to pay.

The two men shook hands, greeting each other without any real feeling of warmth. Although some distance away, Prentiss could hear them clearly from his observation point and listened intently.

"Is everything in place for tomorrow?" Donnelly asked. Noble nodded.

"Yes, I've taken care of it. I have accounted for every

possible variation and counter move. The only way it can go wrong now is if you cock it up."

"And what about that wee bastard of yours? Where is he?" Donnelly rubbed his aching shoulder.

"Under arrest in a cell or shot dead in the process or at least very soon will be. Him and that little bitch that's helping him," Noble reassured.

"You mean you've got no idea. For all you know he is still running around out there causing trouble." Prentiss listened impassively, his eyes fixed on the two dark figures.

"Just relax. There's nothing he can do," Noble said irritably. "Now let's go over the details for tomorrow, time is short." Noble went to his car and produced a large flash light and a map. Spreading the map on the saloon's bonnet, the two men stood together, Noble shining the light as they studied it.

"The target will be travelling by Wessex helicopter along this flight path." Noble drew a line with a pencil over the map as Donnelly watched. "The best place to hit it is here at approximately ten forty-five tomorrow morning." He marked an area on the map with a cross and circled it twice. "This wooded area will offer you some cover and give you a means of escape."

"Won't there be security on the ground? After all, we are talking about the British Prime Minister, " Donnelly asked. Prentiss' heart was racing as he listened unobserved.

"No," Noble said succinctly. "Firstly, it's too far from the venue to warrant making that area secure and secondly, almost everybody is under the impression that she will be flying into Aldergrove by jet." Prentiss wished he could get a look at the map to see where it was they were discussing.

"Have you got somebody to do Aldergrove?" Noble asked.

"Yes ex Irish Rangers sniper Duggie McMahon, he's a good man."

"And necessarily expendable I'm afraid."

"Sacrifices have to be made for the greater good," Donnelly said matter of factly.

"Does he know that?" Noble asked, already knowing the answer was no.

A few minutes later the low hum of a small aircraft could be heard faintly in the distance. Donnelly and Noble scanned the sky and saw the navigation lights of the plane approaching at low level.

"That's our German friend with his customary punctuality unless I'm very much mistaken," said Noble as two large spotlights, one slung under each wing, were switched on to allow the pilot to land on the unlit airfield. As the single engine Lark Commander touched down with a momentary screech of rubber on concrete, another set of headlights approached at high speed from the airfield entrance. Noble took out his gun but Donnelly grabbed his arm and told him to wait. The white Ford Escort skidded to a stop close by the other two vehicles and a young moustachioed man in his early twenties jumped out excitedly.

"He's with me." Donnelly said quietly as Noble lowered his gun.

"Sorry I'm late, Liam," he said apologetically. He walked over to Noble and held out his hand "Duggie's the name." Noble ignored the young man's hand reaching into the Princess and, after pulling out the holdall, started walking towards the taxiing plane. Donnelly and Duggie followed.

The single prop juddered to a stop as the engine fell silent and the three fixed wheels of the undercarriage rolled the plane to a standstill a few yards from the waiting men. The little door beneath the wing swung open and a large muscular man climbed out onto the runway.

Kurt Schroeder was the archetypal German. He was tall with blue eyes and crew cut blond hair although, now in his early fifties, it was more snowy than sandy. Born in Hamburg in 1929, he had been too young to fight in the war but had been a fervent member of the Hitler Youth. Having attended one of the elite training academies designed to nurture the future Nazi leadership, he had risen to the rank of *Oberstammfuhrer* or Senior Unit Leader.

Following a brief and unremarkable career as a pilot in the German Air Force, Schroeder pursued a career as an arms dealer. Having successfully dabbled in selling Air Force small arms on the black market, it wasn't long before he had a reputation of being able to supply anything from a handgun to an artillery piece to anyone anywhere. It was when he was supplying arms to a small terrorist group in Cologne that was under surveillance by British Army Intelligence in 1975 that he met Jeremy Noble. Then a Lieutenant in the Intelligence Corps, Noble had cultivated a secret relationship with Schroeder as a source of credible intelligence in return for turning a blind eye to his activities. Time and again Schroeder had proved to be invaluable to Noble as he never had to doubt the veracity of the information he supplied. The two men had become as close to friends as one could in a business built on suspicion and deceit.

The big German greeted Noble by throwing his arms around him and patting him heartily on the back. "Jeremy, my dear friend. It is good to see you again after so long. How long has it been, two years?"

"Nearer three." Noble's smile was genuine as the two men looked at each other. "You are looking well, Kurt; the years have been kind to you."

"Ah yes, that and the love of a good woman. Her name is Inga; she's twenty-three and a Swedish exotic dancer. She takes good care of me, if you know what I mean." Laughing loudly he slapped Noble hard on the arm.

"You want to be careful, old friend. At your age it's that kind of care that will put you in an early grave." Schroeder exploded with laughter at Noble's reply. Donnelly stepped forward.

"As touching as this reunion is, do you think we might get on with our business; some of us don't have time to waste?" he said impatiently.

"Terrorists are the same the world over, no manners." Schroeder muttered to Noble.

"Liam Donnelly, Kurt Schroeder." Noble introduced the two

men.

"Have you got my stuff?" Donnelly asked sharply. Schroeder stiffened. He could see that there was little point trying to be friendly with this man.

"Have you got my money?"

"Right here." Donnelly held up the attaché case.

From his observation point behind the store building, Prentiss could see the men clearly as they were lit by the car's headlights but found it difficult to hear what they were saying. He decided to get nearer so, keeping close to the ground, he ran to the parked vehicles and crouched behind Noble's Princess. He watched as Schroeder took two crates from the plane and put them on the runway. He opened the smaller of the two with a crow bar. Once the lid was off Donnelly bent down and lifted out the contents and handed it to Duggie. The young Irishman swore with delight as he looked lovingly at the large rifle.

"This is the M40A1 sniper rifle," Schroeder said with his salesman tone. "Based on the Remington 700, it is the preferred sniper rifle of the United States Marine Corps. It has a built in five round magazine and, with a muzzle velocity of 2550 feet per second, it has an effective range of one thousand yards. I have supplied it with twenty rounds of armour piercing 7.62 millimetre ammunition and a ten power scope. Is that acceptable?"

"She's a beauty, so she is." Duggie said running his hand up and down the polished steel barrel.

Prentiss continued to watch carefully as the rifle was put

away in the crate and the second, larger one was opened. Schroeder took out what looked to Prentiss to be a long pipe with a large box at one end. Schroeder carried it in front of one of the spotlights under the wing.

"Now this is something very special," he said to Donnelly. "It is so new it isn't even in service yet. This is the Stinger surface to air missile. A shoulder fired portable rocket launcher that is light and easy to use." He lifted it onto his shoulder and proceeded to explain how it worked. Donnelly listened attentively, asking questions to assure himself that he fully understood the weapon. Schroeder summed up, "It will shoot down an aircraft flying at an altitude of up to fifteen thousand feet with a missile travelling at sixteen hundred miles per hour. With this baby you can take down an airliner." He paused impressively. "Is that acceptable?"

"It is that," Donnelly replied seriously. Schroeder put the weapon away and then faced Donnelly.

"So there only remains the matter of payment. It's fifty thousand for the Stinger and another five for the rifle. In US Dollars, if you please." Donnelly picked up the attaché case, counted out fifty-five thousand dollars and handed the stack of bills to Schroeder.

"It has been a pleasure doing business with you, Herr Donnelly. Should you require anything else, you have my number." With a single sharp nod of the head he shook Donnelly's hand and turned to Noble. "Well, my friend, it is time we were leaving. We must refuel in France and then on to Dortmund."

"You're leaving?" Donnelly asked.

"Yes, it won't be long before I'm discovered, if I haven't been already. I'm going to retire and spend my quarter of a million dollars extravagantly and leave you to your little war. Good luck tomorrow."

As Noble and Schroeder got into the plane Prentiss felt an uncontrollable urge to take out his gun and shoot him right there. He couldn't just let Noble fly away - not after he had betrayed so many. But the plane was about hundred feet from him and he seriously doubted whether he could hit Noble at that distance in the dark. And what was Donnelly planning to do tomorrow with all that firepower? Reluctantly Prentiss decided to let Noble go and to continue following Donnelly and discover what he was planning.

Donnelly and Duggie had picked up the two crates between them and were walking back towards the vehicles. Prentiss, staying low to avoid detection, scurried away past the storage building and headed back to the car where Orla was waiting. He opened the door and got into the car, panting hard. Orla fumbled for the little gun on her lap, taken by surprise at Prentiss' sudden arrival. She lowered the gun, closing her eyes with relief that it was Prentiss that had returned. "Well?" she asked as he sat next to her without speaking. "What happened?" Prentiss hesitated for a moment then replied

"Things have just got a lot more complicated."

Chapter Eighteen

At four thirty-three the following morning Colonel Charles Mabbitt was woken by the telephone ringing in his quarters at RAF Aldergrove. He opened his eyes slowly, having closed them less than three hours earlier to get some badly needed sleep. It was now Wednesday and he had barely slept at all since Sunday. The lack of sleep combined with the stress of the operation was beginning to tell on him. He felt irritable and frustrated and the murder of Katie Preston weighed heavily on his mind. His mood therefore didn't improve as he answered the phone and heard Dominic Fellows condescending voice in his ear.

"Yes, Dominic. What is it?"

"Good Morning, Charles," he said brightly. "Just thought I'd give you a quick courtesy call." Mabbitt was immediately suspicious as Dominic Fellows didn't know the meaning of the word courtesy.

"About what?" he said testily.

"I'm changing the PM's venue for her visit today. She will now go to Thiepval Barracks and not to you at Aldergrove."

"Why?"

"I have received reliable intelligence that there is a credible assassination threat to the Prime Minister by the Provos at Aldergrove. A distance shot from a long range sniper. I have therefore initiated an alternate travel and venue schedule with immediate effect." Fellows could barely contain the triumphant tone in his voice. Mabbitt swung his legs over the side of his bed and sat up.

"I don't know of such a threat."

"You see, Charles, there you go again thinking that you have this infallible intelligence gathering clique when, quite clearly, you don't. We at the Security Service have resources and capabilities far beyond anything your little group will ever have."

"And from where did you receive this credible intelligence? The PM's visit is so secret only a handful of people know about it. How on earth did the Provos find out?" Mabbitt replied furiously.

"Oh I don't think you need to know that, Charles. After all you didn't confide in me over the Boyle fiasco, did you? Perhaps if you had you wouldn't be in the mess that you are now. I'm going to make a recommendation that in future it would be better if you sought operational approval from me to avoid any further breakdowns in communication." Mabbitt knew that if Fellows made a case to the Joint Intelligence Committee for all intelligence gathering in Northern Ireland to be kept under one umbrella with him at its head The Det's operational capability would be seriously compromised. It was its very autonomy that made it uniquely successful at covert surveillance operations in the province. Mabbitt had no intention of allowing an ambitious glory seeking bureaucrat like Fellows anywhere near his unit.

"One of these days, Dominic…" Mabbitt began but was cut short.

"Oh come now, Charles, don't be so churlish." Fellows' tone changed. "Make the most of what little time you have left. It won't be long before everyone agrees that your retirement is long overdue." Before he could respond Mabbitt heard a click as Fellows hung up.

Mabbitt ruminated on Fellows' telephone call as he washed, shaved and dressed. It wasn't possible, he concluded, that Fellows would suddenly have access to such high grade intelligence without him knowing about it. It was all just a little too convenient.

Mabbitt crossed to the phone, stroking his pencil moustache as he did so, and asked for an outside line. It only rang once before Richard Jordan answered. "Richard, I've got another little job for you."

Orla opened her eyes and looked up at Prentiss. She had slept soundly since a little after midnight curled up on the back seat of the Volvo. "What time is it?" she asked, sitting up and brushing her long red hair away from her face with her fingertips.

"Five-thirty. It'll be light in about half an hour."

"Michael!" she scolded "You were supposed to wake me at three so you could get some sleep. You must be exhausted."

"I'm okay, I'm really not tired. Anyway, after all you've been through you looked as if you could do with the rest for a while." Orla had to admit she did feel better for having slept. They had followed Donnelly's van and Duggie's Escort for about an hour having left Cluntoe airfield just after ten fifteen. Once again Orla had pursued them without the use of her headlights until they finally reached a remote farmhouse at eleven thirty.

Surrounded by woodland there was much natural cover to hide the Volvo amongst the trees and maintain a discreet watch on the farmhouse. At five hundred yards they were a safe distance away but still had a good view of the house and surrounding outbuildings. Prentiss had spent the night staring intently at the farmhouse catching the occasional glimpse of Donnelly as he walked past a lit window. Orla rested her chin on the top of the driver's seat and looked at the farmhouse. "Has anything happened?"

"No, but whatever it is they're planning, it's going to happen today."

"Tell me again what you heard." Orla said.

"Noble gave Donnelly a map with the flight path of the Prime Minister's Wessex helicopter marked on it. He's planning to shoot it down with something called a Stinger missile at about a quarter to eleven this morning. But he's also sending the one in the Escort, Duggie, to Aldergrove with a high velocity rifle."

"The RAF base?" asked Orla.

"Yes. Why would he do that if he's shooting down the helicopter himself? And another thing, Noble said that Duggie was necessarily expendable. Why would he say that?" Prentiss rubbed his eyes with the heels of his hands. "I don't know. If I could only get a look at that map, we would at least know Donnelly's firing point." He closed his eyes. "Do you know it was a week ago today that I met them all for the first time - Mabbitt, Noble, Katie - and they told me their ridiculous plan. It seems so long ago. I was supposed to be back home by now."

"Have you got a girl waiting for you there?"

"No, not really. I didn't think it was a good idea to get serious with anyone as I was joining the army. There is one girl I'm thinking of asking out when this is all over, though."

"What's she like?"

"Well, she's pretty, long red hair, green eyes. A bit bossy though and she snores in her sleep."

"I do not!" Orla exploded. Prentiss laughed then held his painful ribs.

"What about you? Is there a funny little leprechaun in Orla Duncan's life?" Orla elbowed Prentiss on the shoulder.

"Aren't you the witty one, Michael Prentiss? As a matter of fact I have young men falling all over me, thank you very much. I'm just very particular."

"Particular, or peculiar?" He smiled and opened his eyes looking at her sideways.

"Do you want another broken rib?" she said wrinkling her nose. "Go to sleep, why don't you, and I'll wake you if anything happens."

Prentiss had dozed for about forty five minutes when he woke hearing Orla calling his name. It was daylight and Prentiss squinted as he focused on the farmhouse. Donnelly was walking out of the house by a side door into the farmyard with Duggie close behind carrying the rifle.

"Day of the Jackal!" Prentiss exclaimed.

"What?" Orla said at the unexpected outburst.

"The Day of the Jackal, it's a film with Edward Fox about a plot to assassinate Charles de Gaulle. You do have cinemas here, don't you?" he said wryly.

"Yes, we have cinemas and electricity and running water." Orla replied indignantly. "What about it?"

"The Jackal has to zero in the telescopic sight on his rifle before he can carry out the assassination."

"So?"

"So if I'm right they're off to do the same with his rifle before Duggie can go to Aldergrove."

"I'm sorry, I still don't follow."

"While they're out doing that I can get into the house and take a look at Donnelly's map." Orla looked concerned.

"Michael, it's too dangerous. What if they come back?"

"Then I'll have to be quick, won't I?" Prentiss opened the door and started to get out but Orla held his arm.

"Please be careful," she implored.

"I will." Prentiss gave a reassuring smile on seeing Orla's worried expression. "And remember"

"What?"

"Watch out, watch out there's a Humphrey about." he waited for a reaction but none came. "It's a TV advert for…"

"Milk, yes I know." Orla interrupted. "Hurry up and don't get caught."

In his Belfast flat Peter Collins lay sleeping following a rather energetic night with the lovely Megan who had more than lived up to expectations. Sleeping beside him, she lay on her stomach, her curly blonde hair covering most of her face. Neither of them heard the barely audible click of the front door lock. Richard Jordan replaced his lock pick tools in the inside pocket of his jacket and let himself into the flat.

Entering the bedroom he raised a single eyebrow as he looked at the naked sleeping girl and the assorted clothes strewn over the floor obviously so hurriedly removed. Jordan sat on the edge of the bed next to Collins and blew gently in his ear. A smile crept across the young man's face and, with his eyes still closed, he said, "You're insatiable."

"You're not the first to tell me that," Jordan replied. Hearing the man's voice Collins promptly opened his eyes and started to cry out as he recognised his interrogator from the previous evening. Jordan put a gloved hand over Collins' mouth and whispered to be quiet. Megan stirred briefly before mumbling "Oh, Petey" as she went back to sleep.

"Relax, Petey. I just need to have another little chat with you," Jordan said quietly, removing his hand and folding his arms. "Your Mister Fellows seems to have got his hands on yet another piece of vital and extremely timely intelligence and I was wondering where it came from?"

"I can't, I really can't."

"Oh, Petey, we haven't got to play this game again, have

we?"

"Look I'm serious; if I talk to you I'm finished."

"In less than five hours the Prime Minister will be touching down on a top secret visit to Northern Ireland. Two hours ago the location of that visit was changed by Dominic Fellows because he found out there is going to be an assassination attempt by the Provos. There is no way that he could know that unless he had a pipeline into the IRA and if that were the case we would know about it. So, you are going to tell me everything you know or…" Jordan took a small flick knife from his pocket and, pressing the handle with his thumb, exposed the four inch stiletto blade. "I'm going to take your eyes out." Collins recoiled

"You wouldn't," he said terrified. Jordan grabbed Collins' hair and held the point of the knife under his right eye pushing gently against the skin. "Okay, okay I'll tell you, I'll tell you." Jordan eased the knife away from the skin an inch. "Fellows rang me here last night about seven. He said that he'd received intelligence from an unofficial source that the PM was going to be shot by sniper when she landed at Aldergrove today and that he would be taking steps to ensure that it didn't happen. He ordered that when I was questioned about it I was to say that the information had come from one of my informants in Belfast."

"Why?"

"He just said he felt it prudent to do so and that it would do my career no harm at all. He had watched me with interest and thought that I could go a long way." Jordan let go of his hair, put away the knife and got up to leave.

"If I were you I would think very carefully in future as to where your allegiances lie. You're mixing with some dangerous people, young man, who will burn you in a heartbeat just because it's expedient to do so." Megan stirred and opened her eyes letting out a scream as she saw Jordan standing by the door.

"Who are you!?" Jordan smiled at the girl as she scrambled to cover herself with the sheet.

"I'm Petey's Avon lady, just brought round his 'Hai Karate' aftershave." He mimicked a karate chop in the air then turned and left.

As Duggie stood in the farmyard and screwed the silencer onto the end of his rifle barrel, Donnelly walked the two hundred yards to the far end of a tumbledown hay barn. He picked up a lawn rake and stuck the handle into a hay bale. Attaching the telescopic sight Duggie, watched as Donnelly carefully put six small plums onto the rake head by piercing each one at regular intervals onto one of the sixteen tines. Tossing the plastic bag away he walked back to where Duggie was preparing to fire.

As Duggie loaded the rifle Prentiss had broken cover and was running towards the front of the farmhouse. From the car only Orla could see both Prentiss approaching the front door and the two men in the farmyard at the side of the house. Prentiss crouched behind some overgrown bushes near the front door. He could hear Donnelly and Duggie's voices but couldn't make out what they were saying. Duggie took aim at the first plum and fired. It missed. He pulled the bolt back and then forward to reload. Prentiss knew that now was his chance and he ran to the front door and slipped inside.

The farmhouse smelt old and fusty as Prentiss crossed the hallway and found himself in the kitchen. He scanned the room looking for anything resembling a map. He opened one of the drawers on the pine dresser, shaking the assorted plates that stood upright on the shelf above. Prentiss froze as one fell forward, just managing to clumsily catch it before it smashed on the slate floor. He cursed under his breath and replaced the plate. He left the kitchen and went into a sitting room that was dominated by a large brick fireplace occupying most of one wall. There was nothing except for a few empty cans of beer and a couple of plates on which were the remnants of some doorstep cheese sandwiches.

As he turned to go upstairs Prentiss caught sight of something very familiar standing against one of the table legs. He picked up the attaché case he had taken from Thomas Fisher and placed it on the table. Opening it, he found, lying on top of the cash, was the map Noble and Donnelly had been examining the night before. He spread it on the table and looked at it carefully. Noble had drawn a line over the Irish Sea to Belfast. The woodland he had indicated with a cross was a few miles east of Downpatrick, County Down.

Outside in the farmyard Duggie had zeroed in the sight and was plinking the last of the plums. "What a weapon!" he kept saying excitedly.

"Come on, that's enough," Donnelly ordered and, to Orla's horror, the two men began to walk back to the house. She leant forward in her seat gripping the steering wheel, willing Prentiss to come out of the front door as she saw Donnelly and Duggie go in through the side.

Prentiss, totally absorbed in studying the map, was unaware of the two men returning until he heard the side door slam shut. Folding the map quickly he replaced it in the case and returned it to its hiding place. Crossing to the large sash window he tried to lift it open, only to find that it had been nailed shut. He could hear the two men in the kitchen as he stood in the sitting room doorway. To get to the front door Prentiss would have to pass the kitchen and risk being discovered. "You need to be in position by ten thirty latest, leave here at eight. That should give you plenty of time," he heard Donnelly say to Duggie. Slipping into the hallway he crept up the stairs and onto the landing. As he did so he saw Donnelly come out of the kitchen and go into the sitting room beneath him.

Entering a bedroom at the front of the house he pulled back the heavy curtains that covered the window. The air was filled with dust, visible in the early morning sunlight. Orla watched as Prentiss opened the window and leaned out onto the stone sill. Downstairs Duggie emerged from the kitchen calling to Donnelly that he was going to put the rifle away and began to climb the stairs. Prentiss looked back into the bedroom. As he heard the footsteps approaching he noticed the long crate the sniper rifle had been packed in on the bed. Prentiss swore as he realised that Duggie would be coming through the door in just a few seconds. He looked beneath him. The overgrown bushes he had used for cover were five feet to his left. Orla held her breath as she watched him climb out of the window and hang from the sill. With a brief glance over his shoulder Prentiss kicked the wall with his foot and leapt onto the bushes below.

Orla put her hands to her mouth as Prentiss crashed into the bushes. He lay motionless for a moment, winded by the fall. In the bedroom Duggie didn't even notice that the window was open, so preoccupied was he with his rifle. Prentiss slowly got to his knees and crawled out of the bushes, clutching his ribs and grimacing with the pain. Clambering to his feet he ran towards the tree line and safety.

A few minutes later Prentiss got back to the car where a worried Orla was waiting.

"You idiot, you could have got yourself killed," she scolded then threw her arms around his neck and hugged him tightly. "I was so worried for you. Did you find what you were looking for?" Prentiss nodded.

"Yes, I found it."

"So what do we do now?" Prentiss thought about Orla's question then replied

"I think it's time we got some help."

Chapter Nineteen

At RAF Aldergrove Colonel Mabbitt sat at his desk. The change orders regarding the Prime Minister's visit had come through official channels and, although she was no longer coming to Aldergrove, the base was on high alert. There were two curt raps on the office door and hearing Mabbitt's customary "Come!" the female uniformed Intelligence Corps sergeant came in and stood to attention.

"Excuse me, Colonel, you wanted to be informed if there was any news about Michael Prentiss." Mabbitt looked up from the report he was studying replying that he did indeed. She handed him a folder which he dropped on the desk unopened.

"Take a seat, Sergeant, and just give me the highlights."

"Well, Sir, it looks like our Mister Prentiss has had rather a busy night," she said sitting down and crossing her legs. "He is presently being aided by a young woman from Londonderry, Orla Duncan. At around four thirty yesterday afternoon, as the result of an anonymous tip-off, the police raided her flat and discovered the body of her flatmate. She had been strangled. In addition, a quantity of Semtex and other bomb making equipment was found together with Prentiss' bloodstained clothing. A warrant was immediately put out for their arrest and their descriptions circulated."

"What do we know about Miss Duncan?" Mabbitt asked.

"There isn't much to know. She's twenty, only child, no criminal record and works as a nurse at one of the hospitals in

Derry."

"Do we think Prentiss met her at the hospital while injured?"

"There's no record of anyone matching Prentiss' description at hers or any of the other hospitals in the city. Interestingly though she should have been at work yesterday morning but didn't show up, no explanation." Mabbitt took a polished pipe from his desk drawer and lit it with a match.

"But Prentiss has clearly been injured; the bloodstained clothes in the flat tell us that." He puffed hard on the pipe. "Go on, Sergeant."

"Well, Sir, they were spotted by an RUC patrol in Orla Duncan's car while it was parked in a service station south of Omagh at approximately seven thirty last night. They managed to evade capture by hijacking a civilian in his car at gunpoint. Prentiss abandoned the driver on a remote country lane an hour later. He was picked up by the police just before one this morning. According to his statement he identified Prentiss and Duncan as the two the police were seeking but said that the young man was English not French."

"Was the civilian hurt?"

"Superficial cuts to his feet, nothing serious. Apparently Prentiss took his shoes when he abandoned him." A broad grin crept across the Colonel's face as the Sergeant relayed the night's events.

"To slow him down, giving them time to get away, clever boy." He looked at the map on the wall to his right. "Did the driver say which way Prentiss was heading?"

"The last he saw of them they were heading east."

"Towards Cookstown or Dungannon." He studied the map. "There's nothing there." He turned back to the Sergeant. "And there have been no more sightings since?"

"No, Sir."

"Is there any news on Captain Noble?"

"No, nothing. He left Ballykelly yesterday afternoon and appears to have dropped off the planet."

"Has he now? Thank you, Sergeant. That will be all." The Sergeant closed the door behind her leaving Colonel Mabbitt staring at the wall map and puffing thoughtfully on his pipe.

By eight o'clock Richard Jordan had returned to Palace Barracks in Belfast and was closing the door to the small office requisitioned for him during his stay. As he dialled Colonel Mabbitt's direct line he thought about the two conversations he had had with Peter Collins. He concluded that the deeper he delved the more confusing the whole thing became. He just hoped that the Colonel would have more of an idea as to what was going on. Seconds later Mabbitt answered his phone and Jordan reported what Collins had told him. The Colonel listened in silence, his face fixed with an earnestly attentive expression. When Jordan finished Mabbitt considered for a moment. "Well done, Richard, you've done a splendid job. I hope you didn't ruffle too many of poor Mister Collins' feathers?"

"No, Sir, he was only too willing to help."

"I'm sure. Now, I need you to help me find Michael. He seems to have got himself mixed up in something but, as he hasn't made contact, we have no way of knowing what it is. I think he's been out in the cold far too long and it's time we brought him in. Find him for me, Richard. He's in a great deal of trouble and I suspect his luck isn't going to hold out for too much longer. Liaise with Sergeant Rawlins based here; she is keeping abreast of the situation."

"Do you want me to work out of Aldergrove?"

"No, something tells me that you should stay where you are for the time being. It's no coincidence that all this is happening the day the PM visits Belfast. I'm certain that Michael has many of the answers we seek. Find him, Richard. Find him quickly."

Orla had steered the Volvo through the trees and out of its hiding place and was driving fast through the narrow country lanes of South Tyrone. Prentiss was now confident that he knew where both Donnelly and Duggie were going and so felt that there was nothing more to be gained by remaining at the farmhouse. He decided the only way he could stop whatever it was the two men were going to do was to try and contact Colonel Mabbitt and give him all the information he had gathered. They were now heading for Dungannon, two miles ahead, to find a call box and arrange for an extraction for them both.

Prentiss told Orla to slow down as they drove down the hill

into Dungannon Town. The last thing they needed now was to get stopped for speeding by the police. Neither of them was happy about having to venture into a town but there was no alternative if Prentiss was to make contact with Colonel Mabbitt. "Why can't somebody invent a phone you can carry around in your pocket?" Orla grumbled. "We wouldn't have to take so many chances."

Stretching out in front of them was the long straight road that sloped down into Dungannon and then up the other side. Stepping down the hill on the right was a row of terraced houses with cars parked sporadically at the side of the road. On the left was a five foot concrete wall standing in front of neatly trimmed hedges and trees stretching to the bottom of the hill. Dominating the skyline ahead at the top of the hill was the huge Church of Ireland, Saint Anne's church, with its towering spire. On reaching the bottom of the hill Orla had to turn off the main road as the main street in Dungannon was barred with concrete blocks. A measure introduced to stop car bombs being driven into the town as it had the rather dubious honour of being one of the most bombed streets in Northern Ireland.

It wasn't long before they spotted a call box and Orla pulled over directly opposite it.

"I won't be long; don't talk to any strange men, will you?" Prentiss said as he got out and ran across the road, briefly looking back to see Orla sticking out her tongue at him. The town was beginning to come alive as it was just after eight thirty. The phone box was in front of a small parade of shops and was located on the pavement next to the road. Prentiss went inside and lifted the receiver. This time he dialled the number for Aldergrove he had been given at Ashford. As he dialled with his back to the road, Prentiss was unaware that their car had been seen by two RUC officers in an unmarked police car. That car was now approaching the Volvo from behind, the policemen inside removing their dark green service caps and radioing in the sighting of the stolen car.

In the call box a voice came on the line after only two rings "This is XNY 556 A for Ares. I need to speak to Colonel Mabbitt urgently." As he was told to stand by he heard a screech of tyres behind him. Turning he saw two uniformed RUC officers in shirt sleeves and flak jackets leap out of a dark coloured Cortina that had come to a stop across the front of the Volvo. With their pistols drawn they pulled a screaming Orla out of the car and, throwing her face down on the Volvo's bonnet, one of them struck her across the lower back with his baton. As he watched, Prentiss was faintly aware of Colonel Mabbitt's voice in his ear saying his name. He dropped the phone and stepped out of the call box. As Orla was being searched, her head pressed hard against the car bonnet, she looked at Prentiss standing across the road. He looked into her frightened tear filled eyes. He couldn't leave her, he wouldn't.

Turning into the road about a hundred yards to his left, Prentiss saw a navy blue Bedford tipper bed lorry. He sprinted towards it trying to put as much distance between the police and the lorry as possible. Remaining on the pavement until the last second he pulled the Browning automatic from his waistband and ran out in front of the lorry, pointing the gun at the driver. Prentiss stood his ground as the lorry screeched to a stop. Keeping the gun trained on the driver he climbed up into the cab through the passenger door. "Drive!" Prentiss shouted. The terrified driver put the lorry into gear and started with a jolt down the road. They approached the police Cortina, its boot sticking out into the road as it was parked across the front of the Volvo. One of the RUC officers was in the driver's seat on the radio while the other was standing with Orla on the pavement next to the Volvo. "When we get to it I want you to ram that Cortina!" Prentiss yelled at the lorry driver.

"What!?"

"Just do it! And then keep your head down!" Prentiss grabbed the steering wheel and pulled it hard. The lorry veered wildly into the Cortina, hitting it just behind the rear door.

As the police car smashed into the Volvo the officer next to Orla fired a single shot at the lorry. It shattered the windscreen before embedding itself in the back wall of the cab.

Almost before the lorry had come to a stop Prentiss was out of the cab and climbing over the Cortina's bonnet. The officer in the police car was dazed and disorientated. As he began to get out of his vehicle Prentiss hit him hard on the back of the head with the butt of his gun. Instantly the officer fell to the ground unconscious. On the pavement Orla and the other officer had been knocked off their feet by the impact of the Cortina on the Volvo. The RUC man scrambled for his gun that lay a few feet from him but Prentiss, having dealt with the man's partner, already had his gun on him. "Leave it!" he shouted as he stood next to the Cortina, training the Browning at the policeman's head. The RUC man slowly moved his hand away from his gun and raised both into the air. "Orla, are you hurt?" She got to her feet

"No I'm okay."

"We've got to go. See if you can start the car." Orla climbed into the Volvo and started the engine. As she reversed away from the wrecked Cortina, the Volvo's front bumper fell onto the road. Although the entire nearside wing was crumpled the car was driveable. Prentiss walked round the car, his gun still aimed at the officer, jumped in and Orla hit the accelerator. As they sped away Prentiss turned to the still shaking Orla. "See what happens when you go talking to strange men?"

Colonel Mabbitt had left his office and was now in the communications centre at RAF Aldergrove. Having got no response from Prentiss, he ordered an urgent trace on the call. Comms was a buzz of activity. As Prentiss' call was being traced there was a flurry of chatter on the police bandwidth concerning an incident during the attempted arrest of a suspected terrorist in Dungannon. As an operator monitored the police band he relayed the information to the Colonel as it came through. "A lorry has been hi-jacked at gunpoint and used to ram an RUC vehicle. Two suspects have fled the scene, one police officer injured; not seriously."

The signals operator across the room tracing the call announced. "I've got it. It was a phone box in…"

"Dungannon," Mabbitt interrupted.

"Yes, Sir."

"Get me Sergeant Jordan at Palace Barracks." In the thirty seconds it took the Colonel to walk over to the operator's station, Jordan was waiting on the line.

"Richard, Michael's turned up in Dungannon. It sounds like he's had a bit of a falling out with the local plods. He tried to contact me here but was cut short. He's still running so get yourself down there and I'll be in touch. Alright, that's all." Before Jordan could answer Mabbitt had hung up and was walking back to his office.

Leaving Dungannon behind them, Prentiss and Orla headed south, staying off the main roads and sticking to the country lanes. Orla had finally stopped shaking but continued to drive at almost seventy miles an hour. Prentiss gently put his hand on her arm and told that it was okay and she could slow down now. She did so, her eyes constantly darting to the rear view mirror. "Did you get through?" She said finally.

"No, there wasn't enough time. I'll have to try again but first we need to dump this car." Prentiss was right. The RUC was implementing a huge manhunt for them and was in the process of saturating the area with manpower, cars and a force helicopter which was en route from Belfast.

"What about that?" Orla asked pointing to a signpost for a campsite at the turning ahead. Prentiss agreed and she threw the battered car into the lane.

The approach to the campsite was down a small dirt road through some woods. Turning off the road before reaching the site entrance, they drove a quarter of a mile into the woods until they could go no further. Prentiss took his Beretta from the glove box, stuffed it into his coat pocket and then he and Orla walked away from the car.

As they walked Prentiss was aware that Orla had become quiet, subdued. "You okay? he asked. Orla didn't reply her eyes fixed on the ground ahead. "What is it?" Prentiss took her arm and he looked at her clearly concerned. "Tell me." Tears began to well up in her soft green eyes.

"Back there I thought I was going to die. When I saw you run I thought you had left me. I felt so alone, helpless. But you weren't leaving me at all. What you did. It was so dangerous. You could have got away but you risked everything to rescue me. Why would you do that?"

"Because you're the only friend I've got here. If it wasn't for you I'd have been captured on the Creggan Estate or shot by the authorities. You trusted me when nobody else would. Orla, I would never have got this far without you." Orla's smile returned. Prentiss wiped the tears from her cheeks and, as they began to walk once again, he added, "although your driving scares the shit out of me."

Just a few miles west the black Morris Minor van slowed as it approached a hastily set up RUC roadblock. As the policeman flagged him down Liam Donnelly picked up the automatic pistol lying on the seat next to him and put it in his front trouser waistband. The roadblock was an unexpected complication and Donnelly considered the distinct possibility that it was for him. The officer studied him cautiously as Donnelly stopped the van and wound down the window. He pulled down his heavy woollen sweater to conceal his gun as the policeman approached. "What's the problem?" Donnelly asked in a matter of fact tone.

"We're looking for two suspects fleeing an incident in Dungannon earlier this morning; a man and a woman. The man could be passing himself off as a French student. Have you seen anyone like that?"

"French?" he said quickly his mind returning to a kitchen on the Creggan estate.

"Yes, have you seen anyone like that?" Replying that he hadn't, Donnelly was questioned further. Where are you going? What are you doing? Where have you come from? The questions were routine and Donnelly was now relaxed, confident that they had no idea who he was or what he was doing. Explaining that he was delivering second hand motor spares to Newcastle, County Down he was asked if he had objection to opening the back for an inspection. The officer used a tone that suggested that Donnelly had little choice whether he objected or not.

The two men walked to the back of the van and Donnelly opened the back doors. Inside the van was piled high with cardboard boxes of assorted motor parts all supplied by Jim at the scrap yard the previous day. These concealed the large transit crate containing the Stinger missile and launcher buried underneath and covered by a tarpaulin. The RUC man peered inside. There was nothing here to interest him. Telling Donnelly that everything was fine and apologising for the delay, he signalled an okay to the officer ahead. Lighting a cigarette Donnelly climbed back into his van and drove slowly through the roadblock. He smiled. In two hours he would be striking at the heart of British rule in Northern Ireland and nobody was going to stop him.

Chapter Twenty

Duggie drove the dark green 1972 Vauxhall Victor FE estate that had been stored for him at the farmhouse north towards Belfast. Before leaving, the sniper rifle had been hidden in a specially constructed compartment in the boot floor beneath the carpet. Donnelly had shook him warmly by the hand assuring him that one of his men would be driving a BMW by Duggie's insertion point at Aldergrove to ensure his escape. A large drink and twenty thousand pounds would be waiting for him when the job was done. Duggie had smiled excitedly as he got into the car, completely ignorant of how the man he trusted had set him up. There had been no hint of regret or remorse in Donnelly's face as he watched Duggie drive out of the farmyard knowing that he had sent him to his certain death. Donnelly had given him strict orders to keep his speed down and not to attract attention to himself. Despite this Duggie had the window open and was singing tunelessly to Going Underground by 'The Jam' that he had playing at full volume on the radio as the estate car hurtled along the A1 towards Lisburn.

Duggie McMahon had joined the Royal Irish Rangers straight from school at sixteen and had been identified as an exceptionally good shot during basic training. Having been strongly advised to train as a sniper by his CO, Duggie underwent the rigorous snipers' course at which he excelled. Learning advanced navigation, escape and evasion together with disguise and concealment techniques Duggie passed out top of his course.

At nineteen he was set for a glittering army career, his skill admired and respected by both his peers and superiors alike.

Unfortunately a combination of arrogant rebelliousness and a smug awareness of his own ability, together with a reckless disregard for authority, resulted in his court martial at twenty one for striking an officer. Picked up by the Provos, who were quite happy to stroke his over developed ego, Duggie now had a reputation for being able to carry out the most difficult sniper attacks without being caught. So when Liam Donnelly approached him one rainy night in the Shamrock Bar in Belfast looking for a professional that could carry out an impossible high profile assassination, Duggie was interested. Several beers later Donnelly had outlined his plan to assassinate the British Prime Minister saying that the man who could achieve that would not only be a national hero but would go down in history. That was it, Duggie couldn't resist the challenge.

It was precisely nine thirty when Duggie pulled up at a remote stretch of perimeter fence on the far side of the main runway at RAF Aldergrove. Twenty feet high and topped with razor wire, the perimeter fence was patrolled regularly by RAF Regiment dog handlers. Cutting the fence with wire cutters he created a space just large enough to crawl through. Then, returning to the car, he jacked up the offside rear wheel and pulled it off, slashing the tyre thus giving the appearance of a blow-out. Leaving the flat tyre leaning up against the car he opened the boot and, casually looking around him for movement, pulled out a sports bag. There was almost no traffic. Duggie knew he would have to move quickly as a lone car parked so close to a military base would soon warrant investigation. He pulled out a bundle of green camouflage and unrolled it. The ghillie suit was a standard piece of equipment for a professional sniper. The lightweight suit made up of several components was covered in strips of green cloth designed to blend into rural surroundings offering three-dimensional concealment to the sniper.

Pulling on the head dress, his face covered with camouflage netting, Duggie took the rifle from the secret compartment in the car and crawled through the fence. Running the two hundred yards to an area of scrubland a quarter of a mile from the runway, Duggie took up position. He checked the time, nine forty-five. Seventy five minutes until his target was due to land. Confident that he had been undetected he settled down to wait.

In a hangar on the other side of the base a troop of sixteen men from the Special Air Service Regiment were on stand by. Their officer, Captain Murray, was being briefed by an MI5 operational intelligence officer, a rather dour humourless Scotsman simply known as Maguire. The radio on the table crackled to life as a voice announced that the target was in position. Hovering seven thousand feet above Aldergrove, the crew of an Army Air Corps Lynx helicopter had watched Duggie conceal himself. Using a high resolution thermal imaging camera they had tracked his movements from the car. As the observer relayed the grid reference Maguire, Murray and his sergeant located it on a large map of the

Assassin's Run

base. Murray nodded to his sergeant who turned and addressed his men. "Load up, we go in two!" As the soldiers climbed aboard their Land Rovers, Maguire took Murray aside.

"Your orders are to capture him alive, understand?"

"We'll do our best," he replied, pulling the bolt back on his MP5 sub machine gun.

The four Land Rovers drove out of the hangar and tore across the base taking up forward positions fifty yards apart, a thousand yards from where Duggie was secreted. He had the advantage of complete all round vision and he watched the four vehicles suspiciously. The order was given to "Go!" As the four SAS vehicles began to advance at high speed covering as much of the open ground as fast as possible, the helicopter rapidly descended and guided their approach.

Duggie remained motionless for a few seconds before realising that they had a fix on his position. Ignoring the helicopter that buzzed his position he flicked up the covers on his telescopic sight and, targeting the driver of one of the Land Rovers, fired. The bullet passed through the soldier's head and through the neck of a second soldier sitting behind him, killing them both instantly. Moments later the vehicle rolled out of control, eventually coming to rest on its roof. The remaining three vehicles were now five hundred yards away and were weaving wildly to avoid being hit. With an effective range of only six hundred and fifty feet, their MP5's were useless. Duggie fired again with calm professionalism. This time, hitting the second driver in the chest. The armour piercing bullet ripped through his Kevlar body armour, the impact racking his body. He slumped forward over the steering wheel as the remaining soldiers tried to gain control of the vehicle. At last the two remaining Land Rovers were in range and the SAS men, hanging out of the windows, fired their weapons spraying bullets at Duggie's position. One vehicle stopped and all four men continued to lay down suppressing fire as the final Land Rover drove straight at Duggie from his left hand side. In a hail of bullets from the oncoming speeding vehicle, Duggie was unable to get off another shot as the Land Rover drove over him crushing him under its wheels.

Thirty miles away in the 'Sunny Days' campsite near Ballydrumman, County Down, Prentiss and Orla had emerged from the tree line and were casually walking through the site towards the shower block. It was a warm cloudless morning and the holidaymakers were emerging from an assorted collection of tents and caravans that nestled between the many oak and elm trees. Immediately outside the white painted block building was the object of their search. They reached the call box and, while Orla waited outside, Prentiss began to dial. Connecting with Aldergrove, Prentiss gave his identification call sign and asked to be put through to Colonel Mabbitt. Within seconds Prentiss heard a familiar voice exploding with relief in his ear. "Michael, my dear boy. It's so good to hear from you at last. Are you safe?"

"For the moment, Colonel."

"Tell me where you are and I'll have you picked up."

"In some kind of camp site. First I've got some information for you that can't wait." He looked at his watch, nine-fifty. "In less than an hour there is going to be an assassination attempt on the Prime Minister. I've got all…" Mabbitt cut him short

"Yes its okay, Michael, we know. The assassin was killed while being apprehended just a few moments ago."

"So Donnelly's dead?" Prentiss replied looking at Orla's tired face through the call box window. Mabbitt sounded confused.

"Donnelly? No the assassin hasn't been identified yet, Michael but it's certainly not Liam Donnelly."

"What do you mean not Donnelly? Colonel, where was this?"

"Right here at Aldergrove. What he didn't realise was that the Prime Minister was never in danger. Both her route and destination were changed following a tip-off. He died for nothing." Prentiss' expression became serious.

"He was a long range sniper, right?" Mabbitt sounded surprised and confirmed that he was.

"Necessarily expendable" he said remembering Noble's words to Donnelly.

"What? Michael, what is it that you know?" Mabbitt asked urgently.

"His name was Duggie McMahon; he's been used as a diversion for the real assassination attempt by Donnelly." Mabbitt didn't reply. Prentiss continued putting the pieces together. "The

PM is travelling by Wessex helicopter to Belfast and Donnelly is going to shoot it down with some kind of a missile, something called a Stinger."

"A Stinger! How do you know all this?" Mabbitt said incredulously.

"Because I saw Captain Noble giving Donnelly the helicopter's flight plan last night when he took delivery of the missile and the rifle. That was what Donnelly wanted Boyle's money for."

"My God Michael, do you know where this is going to happen?"

"From a wood, a couple of miles west of Downpatrick in," he looked at his watch "fifty minutes."

"Right, stay where you are. I'll take care of this. Just keep out of sight and I'll send someone for you presently."

"But I'm only a few miles from Donnelly. If I can get there and stop him…"

"No, Michael. Absolutely not! Leave this to us." Mabbitt heard a click and then nothing "Michael?" but Prentiss had hung up and was out of the call box explaining the situation to Orla.

"I don't understand why you don't leave it to the army. Haven't you done enough?" she implored.

"I have to see this through, Orla. What if the army can't get there in time and me being so close? I can't take that chance. He's just a few miles from here; I have to try." Prentiss took her hand. "Although I have to do this, you don't. I'm not asking you to come with me."

"You don't get rid of me as easily as that," she replied indignantly.

"It would be safer if you stayed here." Orla just raised an eyebrow. Prentiss had seen that look before. He knew it was pointless trying to argue with her. "We need a car," he said, urgently looking around him.

"Do you know how to hotwire one?" Orla asked

"No, do you?"

"No, of course I don't. I'm a nurse not a car thief. I thought you secret agents were trained in all that kind of stuff."

"Trained? You are joking. I'm having to make all this up as I go."

"Alright, genius, so what do we do?"

"We need to find a car with a… key." Prentiss was distracted by an elderly couple hitching their small caravan to the back of a Datsun Sunny. As the couple walked to the back of the caravan to crank up the stabilisers, Prentiss and Orla looked inside the car. The keys were in the ignition. Quickly and quietly they got in and, as the couple finished with the caravan stabilisers, Orla started the engine. "Hold on tight," Orla said as she revved the car and putting it into gear they headed for the site exit, the caravan bouncing and swaying behind them on the uneven ground. The elderly couple watched speechless as their pride and joy careered through the gates and disappeared out of sight.

At Aldergrove Colonel Mabbitt was on the phone to Richard Jordan in Belfast, briefing him as succinctly as possible as time was critical. Two minutes later Jordan and two other men from the unit were being driven out to the airfield where an Army Air Corps Gazelle helicopter was starting its rotors. Having been told by Mabbitt to take one of the 'Bat Flight', a squadron of helicopters used exclusively by The Det for operations, the three men climbed into the chopper and Jordan showed the pilot his destination on the map. As Jordan and his men checked their weapons the helicopter lifted into the air and headed south.

In the stolen Datsun Orla had pulled over to the side of the road so that Prentiss could unhook the caravan. They had only travelled a couple of miles due to a combination of Orla's unfamiliarity with towing anything and the additional weight of what they both now called 'that bloody thing' slowing them down. With it now detached, Orla put her foot down barely giving Prentiss time to get back in. In a swirl of dust they were off again. Both he and Orla were exhausted, hungry and were running on adrenalin. He felt as if he was wading through treacle due to lack of sleep and the constant pain from his injuries was beginning to wear him down. As Orla drove, Prentiss had found a road map in the glove box and was able to plot the quickest route to their destination. Time was short. They only had thirty minutes before Donnelly's target would be overhead. Prentiss watched Orla as she worked her way up and down the gearbox negotiating the sharp bends and long straights of the Irish country lanes, her eyes scanning the road ahead with fixed concentration. He got the distinct feeling she was really rather beginning to enjoy herself. He only wished he had a seat belt.

In the Gazelle, Jordan was patched through to Colonel Mabbitt at Aldergrove. The Colonel was angry and irritated following the telephone call he had just made to Dominic Fellows. He had contacted Fellows to have him warn the Wessex helicopter of another assassination attempt and to alter course. Having been made responsible for the PM's security due to his successful intelligence regarding the failed assassination attempt at Aldergrove, it was Fellows that Mabbitt reluctantly had to call. The information was met with patronising laughter and derision as Fellows accused Mabbitt of sour grapes following his department being proved right about the sniper, sneering, "and him being right under your nose, Charles." Fellows had then hung up, the sound of him tutting sarcastically still ringing in Mabbitt's ears. His only hope now was flying south in a Gazelle helicopter. Richard Jordan was one of his best men and he trusted him implicitly.

"I can't get the Wessex to change course. It's up to you now, Richard. How long till you get there?"

"Twenty minutes. It's going to be close."

"You have to stop him at all costs, Richard, even if you have to put your helicopter between him and the Wessex." Jordan took a moment to respond as he considered what the Colonel was asking of him.

"Understood. Don't worry we'll stop him."

"Good luck, Richard, I'm counting on you."

Chapter Twenty-One

As Donnelly drove the Morris Minor van down an increasingly narrowing country lane he pulled into a field through a gap in the hedge. The ground was hard and uneven and he could drive only a few feet before having to stop. Cursing loudly that he could go no further, he reluctantly turned off the engine. He could see the west edge of the wood half a mile ahead of him bordering the field in which he now stood. Quite far enough with a day old bullet wound and carrying a thirty-three pound missile launcher.

Opening the back doors, Donnelly began to throw the many boxes of car parts into the field around the back of the van. Finally he pulled back the filthy tarpaulin that covered the crate and dragged the heavy wooden box towards him. With the missile already in the launcher, he lifted it out and, resting it on his shoulder, began to walk towards his concealed firing position in the trees. As he did so he checked his watch, ten twenty-five.

Five miles away Prentiss realised that they wouldn't get to the wood near Downpatrick in time if they stayed on the country lanes. They had no alternative than to risk the main road for the last few miles before turning off onto the lanes again. The traffic was light as the Datsun joined the road heading east. With the exception of a few gentle bends the road was pretty straight allowing Orla to really put her foot down. Having overtaken the couple of cars in front of her Orla had a clear view of the road in front of them. That was when they both saw the police roadblock half a mile ahead. She eased off the accelerator asking Prentiss what she should do. Looking at the map Prentiss could see that there were no turnings off before they would reach the two police cars that were nose to nose across the road. "You'll have to ram them," he said

"Are you mad?!" Orla screamed.

"We have no choice. Hit the gas when I say and aim for the middle where the two cars meet; that will be the weakest point." Orla looked at Prentiss and nodded nervously. She drove steadily towards the roadblock; five hundred yards, four hundred. The policeman stepped forward and began to flag them down; three hundred, two hundred. "Now!" Prentiss said. Changing down a gear she straightened her arms as she gripped the steering wheel and stamped on the accelerator pedal. The little saloon roared down the road covering the final hundred yards to the roadblock. The officer immediately stopped trying to flag down the approaching car and drew his pistol. Before he had time to take aim he was forced to throw himself sideways out of the path of the oncoming Datsun. They crashed through the two police cars, smashing them open like a pair of gates. The officers fired as the car sped away, harmlessly shattering its lights.

A mile and half later they turned off the main road and onto a narrow country lane barely wide enough for a single vehicle. As she drove, Orla asked Prentiss if she could ask him something that had been on her mind. Prentiss nodded.

"Back there at the road block and at Dungannon, you could have shot those policemen to get away but you didn't."

"No."

"Why not? They would have killed you."

"They were only doing their job. From their perspective we are terrorists and murderers. I'm not going to start killing them for trying to keep people safe."

"You're a good person, Michael Prentiss. I knew it the first time I saw you in the pub." Prentiss smiled at her.

"Maybe we could finally have that drink we started on Monday night when all this is over?"

"I'd like that." Orla smiled. Prentiss was about to say that he would too when he noticed the roof of a small black van in a field behind a hedge and told her to stop the car. Telling Orla to wait there, he took out his Browning automatic and got out of the car. Crouching down, he made his way back to the gap in the hedge and cautiously looked round into the field. With most of the van's contents littering the ground around the back of the open doors, Prentiss could see right through to the front. Confident that Donnelly was already in the woods he returned to Orla in the car.

"I suppose there's no point me asking you to stay here?" Prentiss said in a resigned tone.

"So the coppers can come and shoot me? Not likely," she said getting out of the car.

"I thought not. Here, you had better hang on to this." Prentiss gave her the Beretta from his pocket. This time Orla didn't argue. He took her hand "Come on, we haven't got long."

Having walked the quarter of a mile through the wood,

Donnelly reached the south east tree line. He laid down the missile launcher and slumped on the ground next to it sweating profusely. Removing his jacket he wiped his forehead and eyes with the sleeve of his pullover. Taking the bottle of painkillers Doctor Hamilton had given him, he opened it, tipping a few of tablets into the palm of his hand. As he crunched them in his mouth he pressed his hand hard against his shoulder wound, grimacing as he did so.

Wiping his forehead again he forced himself onto his knees, bending over the weapon. He had to prepare the launcher for firing. Reaching into his jacket pocket he took out the Battery Coolant Unit and inserted it into the hand guard as Schroeder had shown him. This would shoot a stream of argon gas into the system to charge the missile. With the launcher now ready it was just a question of waiting. From his concealed position he would be able to see the helicopter approaching towards him from several miles out giving him a steady target to aim at. Ten forty-two, not long now. Taking a small pair of binoculars from his jacket he scanned the sky. Then, in the distance, he saw a steady black speck coming towards him.

Having run across the field and into the wood, Prentiss and Orla were now carefully picking their way through the calf high ferns and nettles that carpeted the woodland floor. Prentiss walked slowly, gripping his gun tightly as he maintained the two handed firing position he had learnt at Ashford. His senses were alert. Any previous feeling of lethargy or tiredness had vanished as his heart pounded against his chest. Behind him Orla followed his footsteps constantly looking about her nervously. Ahead of her Prentiss suddenly stopped and waved his arm behind him for her to get down. Together they crouched in the ferns as Prentiss pointed and whispered, "There."

No more than a hundred feet away, just inside the tree line, Donnelly knelt with his back to them. He was unaware of their presence as he looked intently through the binoculars into the cloudless blue sky. Prentiss turned to Orla, his face only inches from hers. "I want you to stay here and keep out of sight."

"Michael I can..."

Prentiss interrupted, "No you've got to promise you'll stay here. I have to know that you're safe. If anything happens to me contact Colonel Mabbitt at RAF Aldergrove. He'll sort everything out with the police. He's a good man; you can trust him." Tears began to well up in Orla's eyes as Prentiss gently touched her face. "After all you've done for me you deserve to get your life back," he whispered and kissed her tenderly on the lips.

"I promise. Please be careful." Prentiss managed a half smile and left Orla in her hiding place. Donnelly had put down the binoculars and was lifting the missile launcher onto his right shoulder. Standing with his left foot forward to balance him, he looked into the sight and acquired his target. The Wessex was clearly visible now flying at ten thousand feet in a straight line. This, he thought, was going to be too easy. Prentiss was now only thirty feet behind him. Using a tree as cover he raised his pistol, flicked off the safety and took aim. Donnelly controlled his breathing, his finger hovering on the trigger. This was for Katie, Prentiss thought and prepared to fire. Without warning the air was filled with tremendous noise as Jordan's Gazelle, flying at fifty feet, swooped over the trees from behind them filling the sky. The sudden appearance of the helicopter at low level and the downdraft it created caused Donnelly to stumble. The Gazelle started increasing in height as it began to turn trying to position itself in front of the Wessex. Donnelly steadied himself again and took aim past the Gazelle at the Wessex.

"Donnelly!" Prentiss shouted. Donnelly turned.

"You!" he yelled, recognising Prentiss.

"Don't do it!" Prentiss warned stepping out from behind the tree, his gun still trained on the man's torso. The two made brief eye contact before Donnelly turned, lifting the launcher high to reacquire the target that was now almost overhead. Prentiss fired three shots in quick succession into the centre of Donnelly's back causing him to arch and fall forward as he fired the Stinger. There was a huge whooshing as the missile exploded out of the launcher shooting into the sky at an angle of forty five degrees missing the Wessex. The trail of white smoke hung over Downpatrick as the Stinger headed out towards the Irish Sea where it exploded in the deep water.

Donnelly lay face down motionless in the grass as the Gazelle landed in a field next to the wood. Prentiss, his gun still pointing at Donnelly, stared at the body of the man who had caused so much fear and pain. Prentiss wasn't sorry he was dead, glad that he had been the one to do it. Not only in revenge for Katie, this was little consolation for that, but to finally put an end to the reign of terror he had enjoyed for years.

Orla appeared at his side and put her hand on his arm to lower his gun. "You did it," she said quietly. Prentiss looked at her lovely shining face that was filled with relief and was overcome with the realisation that it was all finally over. As they stood holding each other, Jordan and his men climbed out of the helicopter. With their arms around each other Prentiss and Orla walked towards the three plain clothes soldiers passing Donnelly's body without a glance.

"Is it really over?" Orla asked

"Yes, I suppose it is."

"What will you do now?"

"Go back and do the rest of my 'O' Levels." Orla stopped and looked at him in surprise. "You mean you're still at school?"

"Would it help if I told you I was nearly seventeen?" he laughed.

"I wondered why I had to do all the driving." she hit him playfully on the arm.

"Look at it this way, the younger we are the more time we have to be together. I want to spend the rest of my life getting to know you." They smiled at each other, more relaxed than either of them could remember being for a long while.

"Oh well, I always fancied having a toy boy." As they turned, Donnelly's apparently lifeless hand twitched. He opened his eyes and watched the object of his hatred walking towards the helicopter. Noble's wee soldier had beaten him for the last time. Now, Donnelly thought, it was time to put this little bastard down once and for all. He had gone from being a mild irritation to the instrument of his failure and he was going to suffer for that. Slowly, very slowly he drew his hand towards his body. As Jordan called to Prentiss as they approached each other Donnelly pulled the gun from his waistband and with a shaking unsteady hand lifted it and took aim. Jordan's smile disappeared as he saw Donnelly a fraction of a second before he fired, shouting a warning to get down. As Prentiss and Orla dropped, Jordan targeted Donnelly with his rifle. Firing twice, the high velocity bullets ripped through Donnelly's forehead throwing him backwards and killing him instantly.

Prentiss got to his knees while Orla remained flat on the ground. Telling her it was safe to get up he put a reassuring hand on her shoulder. Still she didn't move. It was then that he saw the fresh red blood seeping through her jacket in the middle of her back. "No!" he screamed, turning her over and cradling her in his arms. Frantically he held her, calling her name over and over, desperately trying to wake her, willing her eyes to open. But she had gone. Prentiss wept uncontrollably, his tears falling onto her face. Jordan bent down and put his arm around him.

"I'm sorry, Michael."

"It was over, I'd kept her safe. All that we had been through. It shouldn't have ended like this. It's not fair."

"No, son, it's not."

"It doesn't make sense; I killed him I know I did I put three rounds in his back." Jordan looked over as his men searched Donnelly's body. They lifted the heavy woollen pullover to reveal a bullet proof vest, three shells embedded in the back.

"He was wearing body armour, Michael. There's no way you could have known."

Prentiss looked down at Orla and tucked her long red hair behind her ear just as she had done when they had first met in The Anchor only two days earlier. Her little silver cross glinted in the warm morning sunshine. "We never did have that drink," he whispered.

Jordan remained with Prentiss as, thirty minutes later, they both watched an army ambulance requested from Downpatrick take Orla's body. Jordan felt that, for the moment at least, it was better that Orla be looked after by the unit; certainly until things had been sorted out with the authorities. He now sat in the Gazelle and was speaking to Colonel Mabbitt on the radio. He cut short Mabbitt's congratulations on a job well done and explained what had happened.

"How is he?" Mabbitt asked.

"Not too good, Sir. I need to get him out of here; it won't be long before the plods turn up."

"Take him back to Ashford. I'll be there presently."

The helicopter lifted off a few minutes later to the sound of the Sirens of approaching police cars. Leaving Donnelly's body for the police to find; it lay next to the missile launcher that had so nearly and irrevocably destroyed any hope for peace in Northern Ireland forever. As the police arrived at the scene Colonel Mabbitt was addressing the thorny issue of Michael Prentiss and Orla Duncan with the RUC using back channels and unofficial phone calls. Advising them not to pursue any further investigations into a French student called Francois Dupont and confirming the innocence of the young woman, Orla Duncan. He was certain that it was in everyone's best interest that the events of the last few days be forgotten and definitely stay out of the public domain.

Chapter Twenty-Two

The following morning Prentiss woke in his quarters at Templar Barracks near Ashford. The sleeping pills given to him by the Medical Officer were still on the bedside table. He had spent the late afternoon having his injuries treated in the infirmary and what was left of his tooth had been extracted and the gum stitched. Then followed a three hour debrief by Richard Jordan during which he recounted every detail from his departure from Ashford on Saturday afternoon to Orla's death that morning. By nine o'clock he had finished. That was when the unit shrink, Dr Alexander's, head appeared round the office door saying he felt it important that they have a little chat as soon as possible. Prentiss had politely told him to piss off as he was now going to bed.

He was relieved to finally wake up and discover it was light. Each time he had finally nodded off after endless tossing and turning his thoughts of Orla were replaced by the memory of being tortured by Donnelly. Many times that night he had woken from this nightmare sweating and crying out in the darkness. He sat on the edge of the bed and looked at the time, quarter to six. After taking a long hot shower he dressed in army combats and went for breakfast in the mess hall. Having barely eaten for days he voraciously ate a huge fried breakfast, choosing to sit alone away from the bleary eyed Intelligence Corps soldiers returning from an all night exercise.

As Prentiss finished eating he became aware of somebody standing in front of him. Looking up he saw Doctor Alexander watching him with that professional smile he always seemed to have on his face. "Morning, Michael. Mind if I sit down?" Prentiss didn't reply just sipped his coffee. "I'm glad to see that you are eating. You are looking much better this morning." Prentiss just looked at him over his cup. "How did you sleep?"

"Fine," he said, finally putting his coffee down on the table.

"I've read your debrief. You've had a very difficult time during the last few days - far worse than any of us could have anticipated." Prentiss found the man irritating. He hated the way he always chose his words carefully using that 'let me help you' tone of voice.

"I'm fine."

"Michael, you're not fine. You have undergone serious psychological trauma. Your capture by Donnelly, witnessing Lieutenant Preston's murder and the death of your friend, Orla Duncan." On hearing Orla's name Prentiss had had enough.

"Look, I appreciate you trying to help but I really don't need it so why don't you save it for someone who does? Now I'd be grateful if you'd just stay away from me." Pushing his plate away he got up and left the mess hall. As he walked across the empty parade ground towards the sports field Prentiss was filled with rage and annoyance. He was desperately trying to keep it together. The last thing he needed right now was to have some kind of soul searching exploration of his feelings with a well meaning 'I feel your pain' merchant. It hurt too much for that. For the time being he just wanted to be on his own.

Two hours later Colonel Mabbitt was being driven through the London morning rush hour traffic in a Mercedes saloon staff car. Having arrived at Templar Barracks in the early hours of the morning, he had spent the night studying Prentiss' debrief report. Following a couple of telephone calls when the sun was barely up, one particularly lengthy one to the Director General of MI5, he had left Ashford for the capital. As his car made its way through Bloomsbury it turned into Gower Street pulling up outside the headquarters of the Security Services at eight thirty.

Following a brief meeting with the DG, Mabbitt stood outside Dominic Fellows' office door. Entering the office without knocking he closed the door quietly behind him. Fellows looked surprised then his familiar sneer returned. "Here to gloat, Charles?" Fellows had received the report on Donnelly's assassination attempt that morning. Mabbitt raised an eyebrow.

"No, not gloat. Too many good people have died to justify any form of gloating on my part."

"So what are you doing here? I really am rather busy."

"No, Dominic, I don't think so. In fact I don't think that you are going to be busy for a very long time, unless of course you count fending off the unwanted romantic advances of your cellmate."

"Charles, you really aren't making any sense so, if you'll excuse me." Mabbitt ignored Fellows' gesture to the door.

"There are two rather burly gentlemen from your counter-intelligence section waiting in the corridor. They are very keen to discover what you know about yesterday's assassination attempt." Fellows jumped to his feet

"What are you implying? Get out before I have you thrown out."

"Sit down, Dominic, and be quiet!" Mabbitt ordered. Standing defiantly for a moment Fellows reluctantly obeyed as the two men sat facing each other across the desk.

"On Tuesday evening you received intelligence regarding a terrorist threat to assassinate the Prime Minister," Mabbitt said calmly.

"Yes, that's right. Look, if this is some kind of schoolboy revenge…"

"What was the source of that information?" Mabbitt interrupted.

"An informant of Peter Collins, a very bright young man, I'm certain he'll go…"

"No it wasn't; you told him to say that when you rang him at home on Tuesday evening." Mabbitt stared at Fellows impassively. "So my question to you is this, if the information didn't come from an informant, where did it come from?" Fellows didn't reply so Mabbitt continued. "Let me tell you what I think. It was Jeremy Noble who told you that there was to be an assassination attempt on the PM and it was him that told you to change the flight plan and aircraft. What I don't understand is why you would go to such lengths to insist that it came from young Collins' informant and not from Noble. Why would you do that?" Fellows began to sit uncomfortably in his chair.

"Look, Charles, I thought if I said that it was an MI5 informant it would be a feather in the service's cap. I didn't see what harm it could do."

"And a feather in yours, of course. As you say, what harm could it do?"

"That's right, Charles, that's right." Fellows began to perspire as he eased his collar away from his neck with his finger.

"Except for the fact that you were sending the PM's helicopter to where Donnelly was waiting with a surface to air missile, weren't you?"

"I didn't know that." Fellows flustered "I took the information that Jeremy gave me in good faith; I had no idea that this Donnelly character would find out."

"Oh Donnelly didn't find out, your friend Jeremy told him."

"What?" Fellows looked completely nonplussed. "But I…"

"Don't tell me, you had no idea." Mabbitt interrupted again. Fellows leant forward and put his head in his hands as he began to realise how he had been manipulated.

"What have I done?"

"I'll tell you what you've done, Dominic. You have falsified intelligence source material in a conspiracy to undermine and destabilise intelligence gathering in Northern Ireland. You have coerced a junior officer to mislead the Security Services on a matter of national security and you have been complicit in the attempted assassination of the British Prime Minister." Fellows looked up from his hands in a state of bewildered shock as Mabbitt rose from his chair. "In your relentless thirst for power and glory you were instrumental in what could possible have been the worst terrorist atrocity this country has ever suffered. You think you are so clever, don't you; so superior. See where all your manoeuvring has got you?" Mabbitt shook his head in disgust. "Goodbye, Dominic." As Colonel Mabbitt left, two dark suited men entered the office to escort Dominic Fellows downstairs for interrogation.

At a little after eleven o'clock Colonel Mabbitt's car was clearing security at Templar Barracks. He had dozed for much of the ninety minute drive back from London as he too had slept very little since the operation had begun. Walking into the main administration block he was met by Richard Jordan. As they walked to Mabbitt's office the Colonel enquired as to Prentiss' condition. As Jordan reported a conversation he had had earlier that morning with a very vexed Dr Alexander regarding Prentiss' complete refusal to co-operate, the doctor appeared. The three men went into the Colonel's office, Doctor Alexander clearly keen to vent his frustrations. "Colonel, I really must protest. I can't possibly evaluate Michael's psychological condition if he won't speak to me." Mabbitt gestured the two men to sit then went to the intercom on his desk and asked if it would be possible to arrange for some tea.

A few minutes later Doctor Alexander was about to continue

his protestations on the long term dangers of Prentiss not receiving adequate counselling, having paused only briefly when the Intelligence Corps corporal had entered to bring the tea, when Mabbitt raised his hand. "My dear doctor, calm yourself. I fully appreciate your position but what you must understand is that Michael has been betrayed by one of our own. Someone he thought he could trust. It was that betrayal that led to his capture and the subsequent deaths of people he cared about. He has been isolated and abandoned for almost a week. Totally reliant upon his wits to stay alive so it really isn't surprising that he doesn't want to share."

"Nevertheless…" Alexander began again

"No. Leave him alone for the time being. He'll talk about it when he's ready." Mabbitt said firmly then turned to Jordan "Where is he now?"

"Over at the manor on the firing range."

"Right, I'll go and see him. That will be all, gentlemen." Jordan and Alexander got up to leave but Mabbitt called Jordan back. "How's that other little job I gave you coming along?"

"I think everything you wanted is in here," Jordan replied handing the Colonel a buff coloured folder. Mabbitt studied it, reading each page carefully. Turning over the final page he looked up at Jordan.

"Have you got your passport?"

In the firing range down in the basement of Repton Manor Michael Prentiss had been practising for over two hours. Colonel

Mabbitt stood by the door and watched as Prentiss fired seven rounds from his Beretta into the head of the silhouette target at the end of the range. Mabbitt called out to him. Prentiss, deep in concentration, continued to reload his gun and prepared to fire again. Mabbitt called again. This time Prentiss paused momentarily, turning his head a little, acknowledging the Colonel's presence then returned to empty the gun into what remained of the target's head.

As the sound of gunfire died away Mabbitt threw that morning's copy of 'The Times' onto the table in front of Prentiss. A large picture of Margaret Thatcher meeting a group of soldiers was beneath the headline 'Prime Minister Visits Troops in Northern Ireland'. Prentiss glanced at it as he removed the magazine.

"We could have been reading a very different headline today if it hadn't been for you. This country owes you a great debt," Mabbitt said quietly.

"So I saved the day, did I?" He said scornfully. "It wasn't enough though, was it? I didn't save Orla. If I'd made sure that Donnelly was dead she would still be alive."

"Is that what all this is for?" He said nodding towards the target. "It won't bring her back. It won't bring any of them back. You can't punish yourself like this; you are not to blame."

"No? So who is?"

"Captain Noble."

"Oh yes, Captain Jeremy bloody Noble." Prentiss threw the

gun on the table. "Can I ask you something about the treacherous captain?" Prentiss said hesitantly. He looked at Mabbitt, reluctant to ask the question that had been going round and round in his mind since he first discovered the truth about him, afraid he already knew the answer. "Did you know that Noble was a traitor?" Mabbitt's brow furrowed as he cleared a space on the table and perched on it.

"For almost a year every attempt we made to infiltrate Donnelly's cell ended in failure. Each time the operator was discovered then tortured and killed. It was as if Donnelly knew just who to look for. About two months ago we put a man in with a cast iron cover; I mean perfect from top to bottom. There was no way that Donnelly would know he wasn't exactly what he was pretending to be unless somebody tipped him off. His name was John McMullan. It was him that gathered the information about Donald Boyle coming to Londonderry to fund Donnelly."

"What happened to him?"

"His cover was blown before we had a chance to extract him. His body was discovered just before we recruited you."

"You knew it was Noble?"

"I knew it was someone in the unit and yes I had my suspicions about Noble but not a shred of evidence."

"But you sent me in anyway knowing that Donnelly would be waiting for me."

"Yes" he said succinctly. "When Noble came to me with his plan to kill Boyle I felt compelled to go through with it in the hope that I would have an opportunity to flush him out."

"So I was just the bait to catch him, an expendable resource." Prentiss ran his fingers through his hair and faced Mabbitt angrily.

"No, not expendable. Never expendable. I saw something in you at the Selection Centre, a rare quality that few possess; vital in this kind of work. I would never have sent you in there unless I was certain that you would have the initiative and the resilience to get you through." Mabbitt's impassioned tone changed to one of compassionate understanding. "I know you have paid a high price, Michael, perhaps too high but I know that if it hadn't been for you we would never have known about Donnelly's real intentions or gained the evidence we needed to get Noble."

"But you haven't got Noble, have you? He's got clean away."

"For the moment." There was an assuredness in the Colonel's voice that instilled a sense of unequivocal certainty that Noble would one day be caught. Mabbitt smiled "Can I ask *you* something?"

"Sure" Prentiss replied.

"When you've taken some time and gathered your thoughts, put what has happened behind you, I want you to come and join my unit. You are an absolute natural for this type of work, Michael. I knew it the moment I saw you and the last few days have left no doubt in my mind." Prentiss couldn't reply. At that moment he didn't have an answer for him. Orla's death had caused an empty void that had left him unable to imagine a future of any kind. With no response from Prentiss, Mabbitt stood and added "Give it some thought, my boy. I'll arrange transportation home for you in a few days when your injuries have healed a little more. That will avoid any awkward questions." He put his hand on Prentiss' shoulder. "There will always be a place for you here, Michael." He turned to leave but Prentiss called after him.

"Orla's funeral, I don't suppose …?" Mabbitt smiled kindly.

"Oh I think I could arrange that."

Chapter Twenty-Three

Rome's Leonardo Da Vinci airport, although only just after eight on Friday morning, was a bustling noisy hive of activity. Passengers on the flight from London were playing follow my leader across the tarmac and up one of the half dozen ramps into the terminal building. Amongst the tourists and businessmen, a man in his early fifties with greying hair wearing a tan suit strode up to passport control, the rubber heels on his brogues squeaking on the polished stone tiled floor. With no luggage to check he quickly cleared customs and walked past the red and white seating and out to the taxi rank.

Colonel Mabbitt took a pair of sunglasses from his breast pocket and put them on, shielding his eyes from the bright Mediterranean sun. Hailing a cab, he told the driver to take him to the Grand Hotel Plaza. No sooner had he got in, and barely having time to shut the door, there was a squeal of tyres and, in true Roman driving style, the taxi sped out of the airport.

Having determined that his passenger was English the cab driver, Constantine, proceeded to ask if he knew his cousin Gino, the owner of a pizzeria in Birmingham. Replying that regrettably he didn't, Mabbitt wished that Constantine would point his smiley unshaven face forward occasionally and watch where he was going rather than look at him over his shoulder.

As the taxi made its way up the *Via Del Mare* Mabbitt looked across at the River Tiber on his left. In its centre was the

Tiberina Isle where in ancient times the Temple of Aesculapius, the God of medicine, once stood. In a discordant fanfare of car horns, with the huge white monument to Victor Emmanuel in front of them, Constantine careered across the *Piazza Venezia*. The piazza was considered the centre of Rome not only being the fulcrum of its political, religious and social life but also as a point of reference for the city's visitors. Then it was into the *Via Del Corso* and the short drive to the entrance of the Grand Hotel Plaza. Relieved the journey was over, Mabbitt handed a very grateful Constantine thirty thousand lira and stepped out of the cab.

Mabbitt walked into the vast palatial lobby of the hotel removing his sunglasses to fully appreciate the magnificent painted ceilings and the exquisite chandeliers. He could now clearly see why this was described as the finest hotel in Rome. Sat in one of the many comfortable armchairs at the far end of the lobby, Mabbitt saw a familiar face. Richard Jordan, wearing a light grey jacket and white open necked shirt, was sipping a large cappuccino. Having arrived the previous afternoon he had checked into a rather less salubrious hotel on the other side of the city. The coffee he was now drinking had cost almost as much as the unspeakably awful room in which he had spent the night.

Picking up a copy of *La Repubblica* from the table, Mabbitt sat next to Jordan and turned to the inside pages. Neither acknowledging the other, Mabbitt quietly scanned the newspaper. Jordan stirred the frothy coffee with his spoon. "He's in suite three-one-two."

"Is he alone?" Mabbitt asked without looking up.

"A local lovely stayed the night, left about twenty minutes ago." Mabbitt closed his paper and replaced it on the table. As he rose he casually picked up the small leather briefcase that stood on the floor between their two chairs and walked to the elevators opposite reception. Jordan remained seated, drinking his coffee and admiring the rather shapely tanned legs of the dark haired receptionist.

Getting out on the third floor, it wasn't long before Mabbitt found himself at the polished door of suite three-one-two. Sliding the *Non Disturbi* sign that hung from the door knob to one side, he deftly picked the lock and let himself into the room. Closing the door he found himself in a living room. The door to the bedroom was open and the sound of the shower could clearly be heard from the en-suite bathroom beyond. Placing the briefcase on the central table he crossed to the window. Beyond the private balcony over the rooftops he could see the Spanish Steps off the *Piazza di Spagne* looking resplendent with the magnificent display of azaleas held there every May. Turning away from the window his attention was drawn to the desk on which was an airline ticket and a passport. He examined the ticket and raised an eyebrow. One way first class to Kingston, Jamaica dated today. Mabbitt took it and the passport and tossed them into the briefcase then sat in the chair facing the bedroom door and waited.

Ten minutes later the noise of the shower subsided and Jeremy Noble appeared wearing a white towelling hotel robe.

Seeing Mabbitt, he stopped in the doorway. "Colonel," he said moving into the room and sitting on the sofa opposite his former commanding officer. "This is a surprise." Warily Noble looked around the room to see if he had come alone. "How did you find me?" Mabbitt stared at him, his face without expression. Finally he replied.

"It was Michael, actually. He was at the airfield on Tuesday evening. He remembered the plane registration; it was relatively simple after that. He sends his regards by the way. Well, he would if he knew that I was here." Mabbitt was cold, business-like. Noble smiled.

"He's a clever little bugger, that one. I suppose he had something to do with the lack of breaking news on Wednesday as well, didn't he? I knew I should have killed him myself when he called me to bring him in."

"But you gave him to Donnelly instead, didn't you? He's still a bit cross about that." Mabbitt took out his pipe and lit it. "Tell me, did you plan the whole thing or was it a joint venture with Donnelly?"

"Donnelly!" Noble laughed. "Good God, no. He has all the strategic acumen of a bag of potatoes. Once I learned that Donald Boyle wanted to fund terrorism in the old country and that Donnelly had made overtures towards him, I decided to have a little chat with our Liam. It was then that I convinced him that I could facilitate the Prime Minister's assassination."

"And he trusted you just like that?"

"No I'm afraid I had to offer up a few sacrificial lambs first to prove myself."

"McMullan and the others."

"Yes," Noble said without a hint of remorse. "When I found out exactly how much money we were talking about I decided it was probably a propitious moment for me to retire. I had begun to get the distinct feeling that you were looking for someone who was no longer, how shall we say, rallying round your flag. Of course I realised that Boyle would have to go. I couldn't have him finding out that half his money was coming my way. He would have sent someone looking for me and I'm afraid that would have been quite intolerable. That was when I came up with Operation Ares. Even by my standards that was a stroke of genius." Noble eased himself back on the sofa. He was relaxed enjoying boasting to the Colonel at how skilled he had been.

"Why would Donnelly be willing to share Boyle's money with you?"

"Quite simply because he couldn't have done it without me. Only I was able to ensure that the target was in the right place at the right time. With my contacts in Europe I could source the hardware to do the job and of course, as I explained, Donnelly really didn't have the brains to work out the intricacies of such a plan."

Noble stood up, crossed to the desk and picked up a bottle of malt whiskey. "Would you care for a drink?" Mabbitt slowly shook his head as he puffed on his pipe. As Noble poured a good two fingers into a cut crystal tumbler he noticed his passport and ticket had gone. Saying nothing he returned to the sofa.

"You see, Colonel, its all about the art of manipulation; the manipulation of people and events. Take that idiot Fellows for instance; he just made things ridiculously easy. He was so blinded by his own massive ego I was able to lead him around by the nose. I expect that you have dealt with him by now, haven't you?" Mabbitt smiled at the question. "Yes, and I bet you did it personally didn't you? And loved every minute of it."

"So, in your manipulation of Fellows your aim was to have all the intelligence agencies in Northern Ireland at each others throats. The resulting disintegration of trust and co-operation between MI5, the RUC and us would make the gathering of information virtually impossible, allowing the Provos to exploit the inevitable void it would create."

"Brilliant, isn't it?"

"That, combined with the assassination of the British Prime Minister on Northern Ireland soil would destroy any hope for a resolution in the province forever."

"I had accounted for every possible variation except for one."

"Michael," Mabbitt said triumphantly.

"Michael bloody Prentiss," Noble sneered and took a drink. "My plan called for someone who would just go in there and do the job, not start thinking for himself." He took another drink and sighed. "And now, thanks to him, here you are."

Mabbitt leaned forward and placed his pipe in the ashtray on the table next to his briefcase. "Where's the money?" he asked. "Hotel safe?"

"No, no it's here." Noble said matter of factly "The question is how much of it do I have to part with to let me go? I'll warn you I don't have the full two hundred and fifty thousand any more. I have incurred a few expenses along the way what with travel costs, these meagre surroundings you see here and have you any idea how much Italian female companionship costs? Absolutely extortionate!"

"Why don't you go and fetch it and we'll see?" Mabbitt replied sitting back in the chair. Noble smiled smugly and went through to the bedroom. Out of Mabbitt's sight he unzipped the dark blue holdall, took out his Walther PPK, cocked it and put it back. Noble then returned moments later carrying the holdall. Placing the bag on the sofa next to him he sat opposite Mabbitt once again. Mabbitt's eyes glanced down at the holdall then back up to Noble.

"Did you kill the girl in the flat?"

"She was a bit of fortuitous collateral damage. I suppose I could have got out of there without her knowing but it seemed foolish not to take full advantage of such a gift."

Mabbitt was disgusted by such a glib answer so devoid of any kind of emotion.

"And Lieutenant Preston, was she collateral damage too?" he snarled.

"Ah come now, Colonel. Donnelly killed her. I'm getting the blame for everything around here," Noble argued innocently.

"Her post mortem results showed that, in addition to the nine millimetre round that killed her, she also had two unit-issue seven point six-five rounds in her stomach, fired at close range. That poor girl must have been in agony before she died."

"Well boohoo. She stood between me and my money and I had worked far too hard for far too long to have some ponytail stop me!" Noble yelled defiantly.

"There's not a trace of remorse in you, is there? You really are a cold ruthless monster. You have betrayed your country and you have betrayed me. Your callous disregard for human life in the pursuit of greed sickens me."

"You're not going to let me go no matter how much of this money I give you, are you?" Noble said reaching towards the bag. Mabbitt swiftly produced a small silenced automatic pistol he had secreted down the side of his chair while Noble had been in the bedroom.

"Keep your hands where I can see them," he ordered. Noble's hand hovered over the top of the bag. "Very slowly put your hands in your lap." Noble did so then his smile returned.

"You appear to have beaten me. I congratulate you, Colonel. Few people have ever been able to do that." He sighed again. "As they don't hang you for treason any more, I expect you have arranged a nice comfortable cell for me. Not quite the level of luxury I was expecting in my retirement but I'm sure I shall make the best of it." His tone was bright almost jocular. "You don't mind if I change before we go?" Mabbitt gave the merest hint of a wry smile as he observed Noble's supercilious smirk.

"That won't be necessary," he said quietly and fired a single shot. Noble's superior smile changed to complete shock and surprise as he clutched his chest, the blood seeping through his fingers. "Why?" he mouthed inaudibly with his final breath as he fell sideways onto the sofa.

Ten minutes later, carrying his briefcase and a dark blue holdall, Colonel Mabbitt stepped out of the elevator into the lobby where Richard Jordan was waiting for him. "I take it we won't be needing that third plane ticket home after all?" Jordan asked.

"No," Mabbitt replied handing him the holdall as they walked out of the hotel into the sunshine.

"Just as well I didn't buy it then."

Even though it was the last week of May, there was a cold bite in the air that chilled the large number of assembled mourners gathered around the open grave. The sky was dark and heavy, reflecting the atmosphere in the catholic cemetery in Londonderry. As the pall bearers lowered the polished mahogany coffin into the ground, the elderly priest sprinkled holy water and led the final prayers.

Some distance away, standing amongst the elaborate headstones and memorials, two figures watched silently. One was tall, distinguished looking with a small pencil moustache. The other was a much younger man in his late teens. He wore his coat collar turned up to conceal his face which bore the cuts and swollen purple bruises of what had clearly been a recent and quite savage beating. As the priest read a short poem by William Blake, Michael Prentiss looked down at the small silver cross in his hand. "I promised I would protect her."

"There are some promises that sometimes, Michael we just can't keep. No matter how much we want to." Mabbitt said quietly. "By the way, I know it's little consolation but Noble was found dead in a hotel room in Italy on Friday. Some kind of lead poisoning I understand."

"I don't suppose you would have had anything to do with that?" Prentiss asked. Mabbitt didn't reply.

"Come along my boy, it's time to go." As they walked away Michael Prentiss looked up at the grey threatening sky. He now had to come to terms with what he had become and face an uncertain future.

Printed in Poland
by Amazon Fulfillment
Poland Sp. z o.o., Wrocław